Empire of Two Worlds

Barrington J. Bayley

Allison & Busby, London

This edition first published in Great Britain 1979 by
Allison and Busby Limited
6a Noel Street, London W1V 3RB

Copyright © Barrington J. Bayley 1972 and 1979

ISBN 0 85031 312 0 (hardback)
ISBN 0 85031 321 X (paperback)

Set in 11 pt Intertype Times
and printed in Great Britain by
Villiers Publications, Ingestre Road, London N.W.5

By the same author

The Soul of the Robot

Collision with Chronos

The Knights of the Limits

The Fall of Chronopolis

Annihilation Factor

The Seed of Evil

One

The sun was not bright for us that day we fled from Klittmann City, riding at seventy miles per hour across the grey stone plain.

Behind us Klittmann filled the landscape, a stupendous grey castle quarried and raised out of the cold rock terrain.

I had been out in the open only once before, so the scene was a great novelty to me and despite the weirdness of our situation I took time to examine it from this new, unnatural angle.

Seen from the outside Klittmann scarcely had the appearance of an artificial construct at all. It was a vast pile, a rough-hewn mountain. A titanic mass of rock that had risen from the ground in some natural catastrophe, breaking out in slabs, blocks, gullies and canyons, ramp-like slides and roofs. It was all roughened and lumpy, and excess building materials spilled down the sides in frozen avalanches.

Which was as it would be. To the inhabitants of Klittmann the external wall was incidental, unconscious. No windows or doors except the one ground-level portal which was almost never opened. The city was completely internalised. When there was any rebuilding or extension the work was done from the inside; nobody ever visualised the exterior.

Unpretty though it was, for us the view had a not small degree of poignancy. We had no doubt that it was our last look at home. At that, we nearly didn't make it. I was keeping my eye on the upright ring of the portal at the foot of the steel and concrete pile. A police sloop shot out bullet-like and came chasing after us.

"There's one of them on our tail!" I said to Becmath.

Becmath was in the driving seat. He glanced in a mirror, grunting.

"I thought they would. Cops got no sense. Hold on, we'll take him."

He decelerated fiercely to about forty. Soon the cop-ship was pacing us, racing parallel at a respectful distance over the grey rock surface. I saw more sloops emerging from the portal.

Becmath grunted again. "He thinks he can play with us. Chase a mobster out of the city. Feel brave in the open. O.K., let's go." He hurled the sloop round in a screaming curve that took us on a convergent course with the cop vehicle.

We had built the sloop originally to operate in the lowest Klittmann streets where the cops do not usually dare to enter. But we had built it with that eventuality in mind and consequently we were bigger, with more fire-power. The sloop was thirty-five feet in length and twelve feet in the beam, and it was armed with Jain repeaters and Hacker cannon. Becmath was laughing now. Before the cop ship could change course we were sending Hacker shells whining away to smash through the other's armour. Bullets rattled against our plating. Then the cop-ship swerved crazily from side to side and finally rolled over, a mass of junk.

Bec drove in a wide arc, keeping the range steady. A couple of cops were crawling out of the wreck, torn and bleeding. Our Jains rattled out a hail of lead. The cops twitched and jerked, then lay still.

"What about those other klugs?" Bec asked.

Reeth and I were already peering back towards Klittmann. The other sloops had started forward, but the fate of their brothers seemed to make them more cautious. They stopped, then reversed back towards the portal.

"They're staying put," I said.

"I thought so. Well, let's get out of here."

So he charged up the engines and we lit out towards the horizon. Gradually, ever so slowly. Klittmann began to sink in the distance behind us and we were alone in the wilderness. But it was a long time before it disappeared altogether.

The action had kept our minds off the horror of the situation. Now a silence descended on the sloop, broken only by the whine of the engines and the creak of the bodywork. The big balloon tyres rolled soundlessly over the dead rock. We all looked bleakly, frightened, at the deadness that surrounded us on all sides.

So we were thrown out of Klittmann City State for trying to be too big. But where to now? I had a sick feeling in my stomach, like you get when an elevator drops from the top to the bottom in ten seconds flat. Somebody switched on the lights inside the sloop, which only made the scene outside even more dismal.

Grey. Grey, flat landscape. Grey sky. Grey light. Even the air is grey on Killibol. Grey and dead. Nothing grows. Nothing moves. The only life is human life, the only food that which is grown in the tanks of human cities or in the vans of a handful of nomad tribes. How, in this world without charity, could we eat?

When we were well out of sight of the exit portal we stopped for repairs. The sloop had taken a beating in the battle in the city, but had stood up well. We also got rid of the bodies of Brogatham and Fleg, who had been laid out at the back of the main cabin but were bleeding all over the place.

"Bec," I said, "we lost two. That gives us food for about two and a half months, if we half starve ourselves."

There were seven of us left: Becmath, me, Grale, Reeth and Hassmann, and the two passengers — Tone the Taker, who like a fool had jumped aboard at the last moment, and Harmen, the alk, whom Becmath had put in the storage hold for reasons of his own.

"I'm thinking about it, Klein," Bec said tonelessly. "I'm thinking pretty hard."

I had to feel sorry for Bec. For him it must have been bitter, desperate, to see the shattering of all his dreams and ambitions. But hell, we were all desperate too.

"But, Bec," I urged in a low voice, "what're we gonna do? We can't get back inside Klittmann. We can't get in anywhere."

While the repairs were in progress the boys seemed to develop a slightly hysterical hilarity. There's always a kind of mobster comradeship after a close shave; now, though, I think the hopelessness of our position had brought it on. They wanted to show each other they weren't afraid.

Grale opened some cans to celebrate our successful retreat into the wilderness. Becmath was silent throughout it all. As soon as the repairs were completed he set the sloop in motion again, even though the sun was now lower in the sky and it was getting darker. I thought ruefully of the comforts I was used to back in Klittmann.

I dropped into the seat next to Bec's. "We've got to decide soon, while our supplies last. Maybe we could make it to some other city and take a chance on getting in there."

"And what chance would we have in another city — or of getting in, for that matter?" Bec replied wryly. "Cease worrying, we'll make it. We got us a practitioner of the Hermetic Art."

I was bewildered. "What, that old fool in the back? Why did we bring him, Bec? We can't afford to feed him, we ought to throw him off."

"If anybody's thrown off, I'll tell you who."

"But, Bec," I said, staring at the endless, bare landscape into which we were plunging like a bullet, "*where are we gonna go?*"

Bec glanced at me with his hard black eyes.

"Earth."

Earth? I shook my head, not understanding. If Bec doesn't want to tell you, he won't. But I knew we couldn't get to Earth. There wasn't any way of getting off Killibol.

Two

A Killibol city is a lot like one of those termite hills they have on Earth and Luna.

The inside is big enough to be a whole, totally enclosed world. It's monotonous. On all sides there is grey: the cold grey of metal and the warmer grey of stone and concrete.

Our city, Klittmann, is a typical example. Some parts of it are bustling with life, in others there's a deathly quiet. Wherever you go you're surrounded by a maze of streets, ramps, alleys, rickety chasms, buttresses and girders. In the busier districts everything vibrates slightly and dust is always falling through the air.

Nuclear furnaces provide enough power; food comes from the protein tanks. Nobody ever managed to grow food in Killibol's utterly dead, inert soil. By a long, difficult process it is possible to break down the Killibol rock and use a fraction of its material in the food-producing process, and that way they make up for loss and waste; but most of the material in the tanks is recycled by reclaiming sewage and garbage.

The tanks are the most important things on Killibol. Everybody's life focuses around his connection with A Tank. By the letter of the law of practically any city a citizen's right to food is inalienable; the most severe penalty is to be turned outside, into the open where you starve to death. But in practice it's possible to lose your connection and have to try to make a living by scavenging, by performing irregular services, or by crime. The tanks are attached to all the organisations that exist inside the city. The police have their own tanks, the construction workers have their own tanks, and so do the manufacturers as well as the city government. So any of those people might become displeased with you and cut off your connection and there's not much you can do about it because the law is rough and ready in Klittmann. Even if you work for the government, if they fire you they tear up your allotment card.

In Klittmann there are thousands of such people and most of them are to be found in the bowels of the city, in the seedy, dangerous quarter that bustles around the foundations. The cops never came in there much; although they would have liked to, the hard facts of life had created something of a boundary between the domain of the police and the domain of crime.

Well, that gives you a fragment of the picture. A Killibol city is isolated, absorbed in itself — there's no ionosphere for long-range radio and the trading caravans that once in a while set out fall foul more often than not of nomad bands, so there's not much scope for adventure or travel — but it needs to be said that the affairs of a place like Klittmann scarcely vary at all from generation to generation. There's no progress, and no decline. The citizens carry out their work and life habits with a blind instinct, exactly like those termites I was talking about. And naturally, change is something the cops, the government, practically everybody, wants to see least of all.

But I guess nothing lasts forever. Even in the changeless conditions of those big termite hills a man like Becmath was bound to turn up eventually.

The constructional urge in Klittmann is to build up. The magnates and government bosses who build themselves lavish apartments or put city extension schemes into operation always place them on the outer, upper part of the pile. It's an instinct with them. Sometimes their efforts go too far and the new excrescences collapse and go avalanching down the outer wall, taking hundreds of workmen with them. Efforts at rescue are brief and halfhearted; by reflex the people inside seal off the affected section, embarrassed at their mistake.

In general, though, the work of Klittmann engineers is sound. And as the pile masses itself further up, the buttresses and bastions down below become broader and more solid, to take the strain. Parts of the Basement — the vast sprawling district right down in the guts of the city — are little more than slums huddled beneath massive arches of steel and concrete.

Hidden under the curve of Tenth North Bastion is Mud Street. Its name is because the buildings are jerry-built from a hastily made concrete mix that looks like mud. Mud Street is what passes in Klittmann for an outlying shanty town — in fact it looks a little like some primitive villages I saw on Luna later. It's dusty, the buildings are thrown together and badly shaped. The only difference is that the bastion, with the whole weight of Klittmann above it, leans over and seems to press down with a crushing presence. The light from the overhead arcs is a sickly yellow.

Just where the bastion comes to an end, and Mud Street opens into a mile-long metal carriageway that's deserted now, there's a place known locally as Klamer's. You enter the door through a curtain and inside there are tables and wall machines for games like Ricochet and Spin-Ball. Sometimes you can get pop there, too, so the place tends to fill up with addicts.

At that time Klamer's belonged to Darak Klamer, a small-time operator who more or less controlled Mud Street. When I first met Becmath, which was in the games room on Mud Street, I worked for Klamer. You might say he owned me, too. Bec changed that.

The first I knew of the raid was when I heard shouts and screams mingled with gunfire from the main games room. I was in the back with another of Klamer's boys when a third looking scared, scuttled in from the main room to join us.

I didn't stop to ask questions. "Let's get to the car," I said. We left through the back door that opened on a side alley, at the end of which our vehicle was parked.

The raiders had already put a man in the alley to nab us if we came out, but I guess he didn't expect us so soon. As it was I practically came out firing. The bullets from his gun showered powder from the soft stone of the wall near my head, while mine sent him sprawling right up against the back of the alley.

"Let's push out of here fast," Hersh said as we jumped in the vehicle. I remember he was a spry little guy who never liked to take chances he couldn't calculate.

"No," I said.

As we came out of the alley, I saw that two bigger cars were parked on the other side of Mud Street, looking like hump-backed beetles against the massive rise of the bastion. The cars were occupied; not all the newcomers were inside the gaming rooms.

I swung round and crashed the car into the entrance, blocking it. Then I flung open the nearside door and we piled out, back into the gaming room.

There were four gunmen in there. Apparently they thought they already had the place secure. Our customers — those who were still alive — were streaming out the back way. Good, I thought, now the back way's blocked too.

I only had a handgun, firing heavy, solid slugs. Hersh had a repeater he'd grabbed just before we left — as a matter of fact it was the only repeater in Klamer's gang. He sprayed the club with it, shooting down raiders and clients indiscriminately.

The gunplay only lasted seconds, but it made the kind of racket that seems to last an eternity and makes everything confused. Finally I realised the only gun firing was my own. The four outsiders were dead. So was Hersh and the other guy — I forget his name now. The club was empty.

I took a quick look through the front entrance, peering through the car's windows to the outside. The two strangers were still in position. Our vehicle was jammed solidly in the doorway and I didn't think they'd move it in a hurry. So I up-ended a table and took up a position covering the way in from the back.

Just about now it began to occur to me that perhaps after all I hadn't been so smart. I was cornered and my only hope was that Klamer would turn up with reinforcements, which knowing Klamer I wasn't too sure of. I wondered who the raiders were. Maybe they had it in for Klamer.

Something moved the curtain at the back of the room. I fired. A body slumped down, bulging the curtain awkwardly.

Silence. A long wait that strained my nerves. I glanced behind me, at the car stuffed through the doorway. But I felt fairly safe from that quarter. I was out of the line of fire from the door and to come through they would have to clamber with difficulty through the car from door to door.

I was wrong. Even while I looked there was a sudden blast and part of the wall caved in.

I just gaped. Dust billowed into the room and obscured everything. When it cleared they were in, pointing their repeaters at me. And I felt pretty foolish.

They looked around, at the bodies on the floor, and clearly weren't pleased. One of them turned back to me, an expression of sublime unpleasantness on his face.

"Well, well. Look what we got here."

Slowly I stood up, the gun hanging limp in my hand. Nasty-Face came towards me, leaned forward and took it from my fingers. He put it in his pocket and then stepped back, looking at me with a gloating smile and pointing his repeater at my belly.

Just then another figure came stepping carefully over the rubble, knocking the falling dust from his shoulders. They all got out of his way respectfully while he inspected the scene.

Finally his gaze turned to me, and for the first time I came face to face with Becmath. He was a dapper figure a little below medium height, neat and careful in his movements. He wore clothes which kind of squared off his shoulders; his face, too, had a square look to it. His black hair was combed sideways and plastered down. He stared at me speculatively with his small, almost-black eyes that sometimes seemed to glitter strangely when they looked at you.

"Are you the guy who drove the car?" he said in a flat baritone voice. I nodded.

"Pretty good going." He sauntered over to one of the bodies, turned it over with his foot. "Too bad about Heth. He was a good worker." He glanced up at me again from beneath raised eyebrows. "You work for Klamer?"

"Yes."

"Not any more. Klamer's dead. From now on Mud Street is part of my territory."

"You sure think big," I spat out.

Strangely, he appeared not to notice the insult. "Pity we had to spoil the place," he said. "Still, it wasn't up to much anyway, was it?"

"Shall I finish off this klug, boss?" Nasty-Face asked eagerly?"

"What? No, I like the guy! Sitting in my car, the minute I saw him come round that corner I thought to myself, for once somebody around here's got brains. That's pretty rare, isn't it?'" He jabbed a finger at me: "What's your name?"

"Klein."

"But he cost us five!" the other objected.

"I know that. Bring him back with us."

Without another word he climbed back over the rubble to the outside. We followed, me with a repeater in my ribs.

We drove towards the centre of the Basement, taking the old deserted carriageway and then turning on to a newer, busier thoroughfare.

These parts of the Basement were richer and better organised than where we had just come from. Eventually the cars went down a ramp and into a garage. Steel shutters hummed quietly into place behind us. I was nudged out. At the other end of the garage more doors opened. We went through into what appeared by the bad air to be sleeping quarters. I began to get the feeling that I was in the midst of a smart outfit.

"I'll talk to the new boy," Becmath said. A few minutes later I found myself alone with him, very much to my surprise. For this part of the world the room was surprisingly tidy. Becmath lit a tube, offered it to me and lit one for himself. Suspiciously I sniffed it, but it was just plain weed, not the pop-derived smoke some people without respect for their persons take.

"All right," Becmath said. "Tell me about yourself."

So I told him. Once I had been a metal worker. But I had a fight with a bureaucrat on one of his personal jobs and suddenly I found that my card didn't get me food from the metal workers' tank any more. Nobody would help me because the government man had part-control over the tank.

At first I tried to survive by hiring my skills privately. But I discovered what many before me and after me had discovered: that the way down is the way down. I sank through stratum after stratum until I finished up underneath the bastion as a gun for Klamer.

He listened to my brief story attentively, drawing on his smoke every now and then and staring at the floor. Finally he nodded.

"Now you'll work for me," he said flatly.

"Suppose I don't like being pushed around?"

"You've got no choice. Tonight I lost five. You owe me an

awful lot." Suddenly he chuckled. "Besides, now you're on the way up! Listen, I'm tankless, just like you, but it doesn't bother me too much any more. You want to hear my story? I've been tankless since I was fifteen years old, what do you think of that? Yes, I was fifteen when I first came to the Basement."

"But how is that possible?"

"There was a fire in a big new extension on the upper pile. A big fire. My father got blamed for it. It was a great hysterical thing at the time. They shot my father. They couldn't really do anything to his family, but just the same we never drew rations again."

"Was your father the designer?"

"No, he was a worker."

"Well, why blame him?" I retorted indignantly. "Why not blame whoever it was that specified combustible material?" The taboo on building materials that burn is understandably quite a strong one in Klittmann, and is not often broken.

Becmath shrugged. "I know the Basement inside out. I've been upstairs some, too. I know how all these one-shot outfits down here work, and I know how those one-shot outfits up there work too. The whole damned city is nothing but one-shot."

He puffed meditatively. "I've had a lifetime of seeing where everybody goes wrong. Eventually, not too long ago, I was able to form my own outfit. I do it right. We *move*. Don't worry about food when you're with us. Listen, what kind of garbage were you eating with Klamer?"

I made a face. Becmath laughed. "Not too good, huh? I can imagine. Protein tasting like paper, months old. With us you'll eat good. We're close to having the whole undercover supply to the Basement sewn up. It's a funny thing, but there's more of a black market in luxury foods than there is of the plain stuff. That's not the whole of it, of course. Once we got organised, I started taking over here, taking over there. It's only a matter of applying force in the right places at the right time. We're spreading out, getting bigger all the time. Already we own the distribution of pop in the Basement."

Pop is an illegal addictive drug that can be taken in the arm or — even more dangerously — smoked. Where it's grown has always been something of a mystery to most people. Some say there's a secret private tank, others that a government agency grows it. Even if Becmath knew, I didn't feel like asking just then.

Maybe it was the weed which was making me slightly high. But Becmath was beginning to get through to me. He was no ordinary Basement gangster, that was clear. Already he was affecting me in an extraordinary way with a kind of magnetism, a spell. I guess he was just a born leader.

"Why are you telling me all this?" I said shortly.

"I've told you, you've got brains. I can tell that just by looking at you. Men with brains are in short supply around here and I need them."

He lit up a second tube then turned his oddly glittering eyes on me. "You'd better stick with my outfit, Klein, because before very long I'm going to make an empire out of the whole Basement."

Three

Becmath was not long in fulfilling his promise.

In less than a year he was the biggest man in the Basement. Nearly all enterprises were sewn up; that is to say, they paid dues to him in order to stay in operation. There were a few, though, that he left alone. "You always need room to manoeuvre," he used to say.

I saw what he meant when the cops started to get interested, and sent in one of their patrol sloops. They didn't usually do that. They had enough trouble keeping law and order in the upper reaches and tended to leave the too-violent Basement to stew in its own juice. As might normally be expected, their intrusion caused trouble and they retreated with a badly damaged vehicle, but without being able to blame it on Bec. Somehow he lured them into a showdown with the Vokleit Gang, one of the independent outfits he had left alone.

In that year, too, I rose quickly in Bec's organisation and became his lieutenant. Not all of his inner circle appreciated my rapid advancement, but most of them had sense to see that a special relationship was growing between me and Bec, so they accepted it. Only Grale, the Nasty-Face who had wanted to put a bullet in my back at Klamer's, hated my guts for it.

Already I could see that Becmath's ambitions were beginning to look beyond the Basement. After the police raid he told me to design and start building the sloop, like the ones the police had but bigger and better. Plainly he thought that at some time in the future he might have to face them on equal terms.

One day I went into his office to find him smoking weed and brooding. "Sit down, Klein," he said. "There's something I want to talk over."

He often used me to sharpen his ideas on. I took a tube from the box on the table and lit up.

"You know," he said, "it's not only in the Basement they got gangsters. They got gangsters upstairs too."

"What, you mean some of those government bosses?"

He waved his hand. "Them too, but that's not what I meant. There are private interests, private empires just like we got down here. Only they can throw their weight around with no sweat. Because the basis of real power lies upstairs, and they've got it.

"You know what I mean, Klein," he added, staring at me with his steady black eyes. "I mean the tanks."

"You certainly can't do much unless you can eat," I muttered.

"That's right. Have you ever wondered about something, Klein? Have you ever wondered why nothing ever changes in Klittmann? Why we do everything in the same way we did it generations ago?"

His remark puzzled me. I shrugged. "Why, no. What other way is there?"

"That's right, what other way." For some moments he sat gazing at the nerve-calming smoke that plumed up from the end of the tube he was holding. "You know, it was centuries ago, maybe a thousand years ago, that men came from Earth and settled on Killibol. They came at the peak of an age of science and technology. An age of great change."

"I didn't know that." To tell the truth I had difficulty even in comprehending it.

"Few do. But as soon as the cities rose and the gateway from Earth was closed, something happened. Everything petrified, even technology and engineering, and we finished up with what we got today — stasis. There isn't systematic knowledge any more, only habitual techniques handed down from generation to generation. I've got a theory as to why that happened. Firstly, the need for food comes before everything else. The tanks are a stranglehold that stops people from altering anything — especially since they are more or less in the hands of a few and the others are beholden to those few. You can't think about anything if in thinking about it you endanger your protein supply. Secondly, the fact that Killibol is a dead world causes each city to bunch up in itself and prevents traffic between them. It wasn't like that on Earth. There was food everywhere and the cities all had intercourse with one another all the time. It must have been real lively. Maybe you need that intercourse between cities to get things moving."

"How do you know all this, Bec?"

"I've read books." He picked up an ancient, dog-eared volume that was lying on the table. "There's a guy comes down into the Basement looking for pop. Tone, they call him: Tone the Taker. He's quite a strange fellow. He knows a place where he gets all these old books and I make him bring them in exchange for pop."

Slowly Bec got to his feet and put the book away in a cupboard. "Wouldn't it be a fine thing, Klein, if people could be freed of their slavery to the tanks?"

"That's impossible."

"So it is. But maybe the stasis would be broken if the tanks didn't have bosses — that's where the real stranglehold lies. Supposing Klittmann was ruled by a rod of iron, by a real strong king or dictator, like they had on Earth thousands of years ago, and the tanks were made available to all. State property, like they were supposed to be when Klittmann was founded? Maybe we could even move in on some of the other cities."

"Is this what you wanted to talk to me about, boss?" While I could just barely get the drift of what he was saying, I didn't at that time see what it had to do with me.

He cast me a sardonic glance and I sensed he was disappointed in me.

"No. We've taken over the Basement, but we're not going to stop with the Basement. Those big shots upstairs aren't so big once you take their protein tanks away. Klein, we need a tank."

His words practically stopped my mind. I saw for the first time that Bec's theorising came to a practical point. But it seemed such an enormous step that I just couldn't encompass it.

"Bec — *how*?" I goggled.

"You see?" he retorted with a grimace, "You can't even imagine it. You think of yourself as tankless, as a gunman living outside the law. But what is the law? It's a gun, it's a mob, just like us. Once we've got what they've got, we can take the whole damned city."

"You sure talk big."

"Somebody round here has to. Now listen, you want to know how we'll do it. It's not nearly as hard as it sounds. Is the sloop ready?"

"Yes." I had, in fact, tried out the new vehicle a few days before.

"Good, we'll need it. There's a guy called Blind Bissey. He owns a tank, just one, located secretly in one of the quiet quarters on the level just above us. Because of it he's able to run a few factories, have a staff around him, trade, live in style, things like that."

Bec's arguments were beginning to impress me. "Hell, isn't that just what we do?"

"That's right. Tone the Taker knows where the tank is. As a matter of fact, it's right close by his store of old books. That's another reason why I want to go up there. Here's what we'll do. One night we'll drive up there by a planned route — and take over the tank." He raised his eyebrows as he spoke the last words. "Simple."

My head was singing with the audacity of it all. "We'll never get away with it!"

"Why not? If it looks like we can't hold the place we'll round up the technicians and bring them down here, and take as much organic material from the tanks as we can and bring that down here as well. That's all you need, remember: organic material and know-how. We'll set the tank up anew in the Basement. Meanwhile I'll get in touch with Blind Bissey and offer him a partnership."

"It's war," I said with a feeling of foreboding. "We'll be smashed into the ground."

"You think so? Where's Bissey without his tank? He'll want it back so bad he'll give me fifty per cent to get it. He'll even call off the cops to get it. I tell you, basically he's a mobster like us. So Bissey's outfit will be our first step on the way to real influence. Once we're upstairs we'll start to edge in on the workers' unions, take over more tanks, form alliances in the government and even the cops. Given time, there won't be anybody who can stop us."

"You seem to have it all worked out," I admitted.

He smiled. "I've read a lot of books, Klein. Some of the people who lived ages ago were pretty smart."

The sloop purred smoothly along the gleaming metal street, taking the regular right curves with barely a whisper. Behind us followed three smaller cars to complement the gunmen who were crammed into the big vehicle.

The district was quiet, almost deathly. On either side of the broad avenue the structures presented a continuous façade that swept up to join perfectly with the roof overhead, dully visible behind the glare of the street lights. Bec had had the route reconnoitred pretty thoroughly; we knew there would be no police patrols along at this hour and we were reckoning on a smooth operation.

Each vehicle towed a big square vat. The four of them wouldn't enable us to carry away all the contents of the tank with us if need be, but they would give us a good part of it; and organics are the most precious thing there is on Killibol.

Becmath drove. In the seat next to him was Tone the Taker, a skinny, nervous individual who had taken pop in the arm before we set out. Pop addicts nearly always go to pieces if they're without their supply. Their nervous systems need it.

Crowded in between the driving seat and the main troop force were myself and Reeth, another of Bec's inner circle. Reeth was slight-bodied, slick and nimble. Becmath had chosen him well. He kept his eyes skinned and alone of all the henchmen he was sometimes openly critical of his boss's decisions, a quality which Bec seemed to value.

"Slow here," Tone said, "there's a hidden turning on your right."

As the sloop slowed to a dawdle we saw an arch closed off with a big sheet of steel. It could be opened, Tone had explained, only from the inside, but that, of course, would not detain us long. We had brought impact explosives with us, the same that are used to punch out odd-shaped sheets of metal.

In less than a minute the stuff was taped in place. There was a short, sharp bang and a piece of steel clanged to the floor, leaving a hole large enough for a man to get through.

Tone stepped inside and shortly afterwards the arch's door slid upwards and disappeared.

Our convoy bumped in darkness down a sloping, uneven surface. Tone instructed us to stop. We got out and proceeded on foot by the light of hand-lamps.

I felt an irrepressible excitement. Never before had I seen one of those places where they make food; I felt, in fact, a vague kind of mystique about it, like you would about your own mother's womb. No wonder, I thought, that the tank controllers had found it easy to hang on to them and make other men subservient by means of them. It took a man like Becmath to overcome that unspoken feeling of reverence and claim a tank for himself.

Suddenly Tone flung open a door and we were there. Faces turned towards us in bewilderment as we blundered in, handguns and repeaters darting about on the look-out for trouble.

There wasn't much to see. We were in a gallery, not very large — maybe twenty or thirty feet long — one wall of which was covered with dials and switches. At either end were doors leading to the culture banks.

We herded the shocked technical crew to the far end. Out of curiosity I opened one of the doors and peered in. The light was dim and the air had a dank, musky smell. There were a number of short corridors. And that was all. The tank itself, I knew, was sealed.

I closed the door again. "What now?" I asked Bec in a low tone.

"Better not try to hold this place," he said. "We could, for a while, but what then? We'll get a better bargaining position from our own territory."

He called over Tone. "You said we could drain nutrient fluid off. Are you still sure?"

"Yes, if we get the crew to help us."

"They'll help us," Bec said, with one glance at the frightened technicians. They wore long white gowns and white gloves. I'd never seen a costume like that before.

Underneath the gallery there was a valve where the organics from the tank could be drained off. Apparently they used it regularly in order to clean out wastes and replenish the nutrient fluid from recycled material in an adjoining chamber.

The technicians were reluctant at first; they took quite a knocking about before we persuaded them to co-operate in opening the valve. The stuff that came gushing out was thick and slimy and the smell was so strong it made us gag. We started to fill up the vats. In spite of the smell we were all excited, like kids, because we were doing something that had never been done before.

"O.K.," Bec said to Tone while the work was going on. "Now take me to this old man."

Tone led the way to the exit. "You come too, Klein," Bec told me. "I'd like you to see this."

We went part way back up the ramp in the darkness. Tone found a smaller passage that went off at right angles and then curved round in a crazy spiral. Shortly light shone round the edges of a thick door. Tone thumped on it with his fist.

"Open up, Harmen," he cried in his reedy voice. "It's me, Tone."

After a brief shuffling noise from the other side, the door swung open. An old man stood there. His hair was unkempt and down to his shoulders. He was tall, thin, but still energetic and hardly stooped at all. His face made an impression on you the instant you saw it: the nose was bony and hooked, the corners of the mouth turned down, and the eyes were intense and penetrating. But the corners of those eyes were wrinkled with humour-lines, and somehow the total effect was kindly despite its bizarreness.

"I've brought some friends; they wanted to meet you," Tone told him.

Harmen's eyes followed us with displeasure as we walked into the room. "I told you never to bring anyone here."

"You should never trust a taker," Bec told him with a smile.

Even before the door opened I had heard a faint buzzing noise. Now it was louder, but intermittent. The air was heavy with the smell of electricity and unidentified substances. The room was large. The light was erratic, and came mainly from various instruments that gave off illumination in irregular pulses and flamed colour against the walls and ceiling.

These instruments were set up on a number of tables. The

whole effect was weird, unbelievable. Something started to creep up my spine.

"Harmen used to be a tank technician," Bec murmured to me. "All the time, though, he was interested in something else, as you can see. When he retired he set up this little place here. It's perfect for him, as you can see. Nice and private. Only Tone knew about it — Harmen was sorry for him and helped him get pop."

"He's an *alchemist*," I whispered. "What the hell are we doing here?"

I'd heard of alchemists — alks — before, but naturally never seen one. They were something you threatened your children with. They were supposed to have evil magic powers and to indulge in nasty habits like sucking the blood from live babies. I didn't know they really existed any more, but of course it would have to be in secret. There were city ordinances against "unauthorised or secret experimentation", and popular fear of alks was strong.

"Alchemy is the only field of scientific endeavour left in the world," Bec said quietly, trying to calm me. "Don't believe what you hear about alks. Harmen doesn't drink blood, and he can't take away your will and make you his puppet by remote control. At least, I don't think he can." He gazed around him. "Just look at all this stuff! I bet this guy knows more electronics than anybody in the city."

Some of the apparatus on the tables seemed to be modelled on discharge tubes of various shapes and sizes, some globular, some retort-shaped with several electrodes discharging into the same chamber. What was going on in those discharge tubes was weird, frightening, but kind of beautiful. Colours — all the colours you can think of. The discharge tubes — flasks, or whatever — seemed to have various substances in them which the electrical charges were acting on. In one, the stuff was splashing against the sides of the retort in colour changes of a definite sequence: black, red, white, then yellow with brilliant islands of green, then deep purple. It was hypnotic. I tore my eyes away, suddenly remembering the stories about how an alk can steal your will and put it in a little mechanical doll.

"What do you want here?" the alk demanded in gravelly tones.

"We've come to see what you can do, old man. What you know." I sensed that Bec was unexpectedly discomfited in these new surroundings. He suddenly felt himself to be a clumsy mobster.

"You want instruction in the Hermetic Art?" Harmen seemed puzzled and wary.

"It's on the level," Tone said brightly. "They're not here to bust you."

"That's right," Bec answered. "Come on, tell us about it."

While they were talking I noticed a screen in one corner of the room. The loud buzzing noise was coming from behind it. So I stepped over and peeped behind it.

There was a big, round globe. Every time the irregular buzzing noises sounded a massive jolt of power must have been flashed into it, because it boiled and glared with a brightness I'd never experienced before. Momentarily I was blinded. I staggered back, blinking. Harmen was expounding to Bec in high-flown language.

"Alchemy, or the Hermetic Art," he said, "is the eternal science, older than any others and continuing after they die. With every exoteric advance in knowledge the alchemical operations can be refined and perfected further, the missing techniques can be devised anew and so the Great Work carried further forward on the path to completion."

"And what would completion be?"

Harmen frowned slightly. "You want answers all at once? My own teacher did not divulge that until I had mastered four separate disciplines of experimentation."

"So what? Tell me now."

"You think it will help you? The aim of the Work is the Tincture, the Prima Materia, Hyle, the Sublime Substance that is neither mass nor energy and by the possession of which one can conquer space and time."

Bec met this proclamation with a blank look. A faint derisory smile appeared on Harmen's face.

The alk continued to drone on, but it was clear that Bec soon lost the drift for he suddenly interrupted: "Is it right that Tone got all those books from you?"

The other nodded. "I have amassed a fair library. Those history books I'm not interested in and didn't mind parting with. The science and technology books I keep. The techniques that are applied to alchemy now come from the science that was developed about eight hundred years ago."

He showed Bec a thick, ancient volume that he took out of a drawer. Stamped on the cover in old-style video-comp lettering was the title: *Plasma Physics and the Secret Art.*

"My library, however, extends right back to the primitive state of the art, beginning with the *Emerald Table* and containing such valuable works of instruction as *The Sophic Hydrolith.* I can carry a process through six stages, from the Raven's Head to the Blood of the Dragon. But not, alas, to the Tincture. However, those operations refer to the preatomic stage of alchemy. The later manuals, such as the *Plasma Physics* and the texts on the dissociation of matter by high-frequency magnetic fields, have greatly extended the range of alchemical operations."

I got the idea that Harmen was so pleased to talk about his work that it didn't matter much to him that none of us grasped too well what he was talking about. Bec cut off the flow of words with a wave of his hand.

"O.K., Harmen, you've got me convinced. How would you like to quit this place and come and do your work in my outfit. I'll give you anything you need — anything. You must run short of equipment the way you are now."

Harmen nodded. "I do. But what are your reasons?"

"I'm interested in original research. The world's gone too long without anything new. I aim to change that."

The alk pursed his lips. "The final preparation of the tincture requires the use of an atomic furnace. I am without one. Can you provide it?"

Bec thought for a moment. "We should be able to handle that." The hardest part of building the sloop had been acquiring its nuclear power unit. But we had done it, so I guessed we could do it twice.

"Then I'll think about it. Come and see me again in a few days."

"Sorry, old man, this is the time for snap decisions." He turned to me. "Get back to the tank, Klein, and send down some of the boys to help Harmen crate up his equipment and books. I don't think we'll be able to come back later."

Harmen let out a roar of indignation, but it was too late for him to do anything about it. Bec had taken to him, for some reason. He was being hi-jacked, like the tank technicians.

I went back to where they were working under the control gallery. The stench was awful. They had filled up the vats and then had found some containers on the premises and filled those. Bissey's tank was only a small one that fed no more than a few thousand people, but by the time they'd finished they had still only drained off slightly more than a third of its hoard of organics. We'd have to be content with that. As it was the technicians were protesting shrilly about the risk of contaminating the nutrient and ruining it.

I sent some boys down to Bec. Half an hour later they came back carrying loads of junk and books and stuff, then went back for more. There was masses of it and we had to leave a lot behind. Then Harmen came, looking wild-eyed and fierce. I told myself it was lucky I gave the sloop a lot of storage space. As it was we left a lot of stuff lying around the floor.

It was quite a while before we pulled out. Outside, the curving crescent of the street was still empty. We jammed Harmen and the six techs in the sloop with us and set off back to the Basement.

The chief tech was yelling that we were mad, criminally mad. "And why are you taking *us*?" he asked shrilly, though surely he could guess.

Bec spoke over his shoulder from the driving seat. "Calm down. You'll be all right. I'll set you up, you can grow food just like you did before. I'll treat you better than Blind Bissey ever did."

"You fool!" the technician fumed. "You don't think the protein that's grown in a tank is eatable, do you? It's raw, you'd vomit if you tasted it. It has to be processed further to make the food you know."

"Then process it. We'll get you everything you need."

Now we were already entering the Basement. The technicians peered through the windows at the dusty chaos. Most of them had probably never been down here before. A stranger to Klittmann might not notice the difference between that and the more select surroundings they were used to, but when you've been brought up in something all your life fine differences are important. Their faces were sour.

We drove straight to the fortified garages and locked up the technicians under guard. Then Bec made for his office, taking me in tow.

In his office Bec had a vision phone, one of the few in the whole of the Basement. He flicked out a number on the dial. There was a quiet whirr of machinery as the mechanical disc scanners spun, one set televising Bec's face and the other tracing a blur of illumination on the paper receiving screen.

The first face that appeared on the screen was that of a servant girl. Bluntly Bec told her of his wish to speak to her master. Something in his tone must have got through to her, because she turned away and did something at a table and her image vanished.

"Bissey speaking," a whispering voice said. But to Bec's annoyance — he was proud of his vision phone — no picture appeared.

"Show yourself, Bissey, I like to see who I'm talking to," he demanded.

"I can't see you anyway. Why should you see me? What do you want?"

"Better come through and show me your face," Bec told him. "It's about your tank."

There was a pause, then the screen's fuzzy brightness cleared and it showed a low-quality picture of a fat man sitting in an armchair. His head was raised, his eyes clearly sightless. With one hand he fondled a dog that he used to guide him when he walked.

"Here I am then. What's this about the tank?"

Brusquely, brutally, Bec told him what we had done. The fat man's face went drawn and pale. At first he simply didn't believe us. Bec invited him to check for himself. When he had done so he was shaking.

"You klugs!" he whispered, his voice shaking. "There are laws in this city. The police department will come down there and mash you into little pieces."

"Sure, let them do that," Bec said gaily. "Give them a call.

But you can say goodbye to your protein nutrient. We'll make sure that's never usable again if the cops look like busting us."

True, Bissey still had two thirds of his stock; but the loss of even one third was plainly a traumatic threat to him. Nothing like this had happened for generations.

"What do you want?" he hissed.

"Listen," Bec told him, "and listen good. We want fifty per cent. . . ."

He spoke on, his words punching like blows into the blind man's flesh. By the time he had finished Bissey was beaten.

Becmath was riding high. He had everything going for him, and he knew it. For him it was a high spot in his life that looked even better because he thought it was only a beginning.

Bissey had capitulated. At first he had wanted the nutrient returned to his tank, but Bec had thought better of it and refused. So at great expense a little tank was set up in the Basement. It didn't make eatable food, only raw protein that was shipped upstairs.

The alchemist was installed pretty good, too. Bec gave him a work-room — he called it a "laboratory" — in the system of garages and apartments where the gang operated from. Anything he wanted, he and Bec used to go upstairs together and get it somehow. The atomic furnace we were still working on.

Soon his "laboratory" was full of spluttering, flashing and buzzing and other noises and sights I wouldn't really know how to describe. I didn't like to go in there. Sometimes there were strange vibrations in the air that seemed to get right inside my mind and make me dizzy and give me peculiar feelings. But Bec used to talk to Harmen for hours at a time.

Bec used to go upstairs and see Blind Bissey sometimes, too. He was planning to move in the upper world of big power blocs, and he liked to sound Bissey out about it. The fat man hated us, of course, but he used to keep himself well under control, fondling his dog, his blind eyes staring into space.

We were on one of those visits when our plans collapsed around our ears.

That day I had wondered why Bissey seemed pleased to see

us for once. He even smiled. And I didn't like the smug look on his face when he said goodbye.

On the way back Bec wanted to stop off to buy something. He had a purchasing card now, one of those issued by the big manufacturing cartels, and he got a kick out of using it. So we stopped the car and went into a distributing outlet. Bec spent a long time choosing a metal belt with designs embossed on it.

When we came out, police sloops were sweeping past, heading for the Basement. A lot of them. Bec frowned, and I had a sinking feeling in the pit of my stomach.

"Let's see what's going on," he said gruffly.

When the convoy had passed we made for home, taking a side route for safety's sake.

Noise is something everyone in Klittmann gets used to from birth. Because it's just one massive enclosed space, sound travels easily and long. We were scarcely within the region of the Basement before we heard the sound of gunfire and explosions.

It was the latter that frightened me. Explosives are almost never used in Klittmann except in tightly controlled conditions — certainly not in fighting. The danger of structural damage to the city is too great. That was why Bec's use of a grenade at Klamer's had taken me so much by surprise. Bec looked at me meaningfully. We went on a little further, then pulled up. We got out and went into a store owned by a trader named Klepp, usually a mine of information.

"What's going on?" Bec demanded aggressively. "Have you heard anything?"

"Something big's happening," Klepp said warily. "The cops are here in force. Not only that but some kind of private armed militia. Not only that. . . ." he trailed off.

"Come on, give!" Bec clenched his fist angrily, his eyes blazing.

"A lot of the old small outfits in the West Section have come to life and formed a consortium against you. It's a rebellion, Bec. They're coming at you from all sides."

Bec growled a curse and strode from the shop.

We stood outside. "Bissey knew about this," he said furiously. "He was just playing us along. Let's go and see what's happening at the garage."

As we drew nearer the sounds of fighting grew louder. We approached cautiously. There was fighting elsewhere in the Basement, too — strangers from upstairs in unfamiliar uniforms were wandering about uncertainly and shooting into various buildings.

"I'll bet those are Bissey's own workers," Bec said. "Armed just for the occasion, told they're fighting for their rations. This thing has been well planned."

We left the car about half a mile from the garage and went forward on foot to take a look. Police sloops were parked in the approach to the main frontage. The lid was down — the big slab of metal and concrete that we had grandiosely installed to keep out an army. Our own gun positions were silent and the sloops were firing Hacker shells at the lid to break it up.

"They'll be through there before long," Bec mused. "Come on, we'll get in the back way."

It didn't take us long to work our way round and get into the complex by the hidden back entrance. Inside, it was organised desperation. They had put up makeshift barriers to hold off the cops when they broke through the lid. Half the mob had already sneaked off.

Grale and Reeth were running things. "We've been waiting for you," Grale said thankfully when Bec appeared. "What do we do, fight or run?"

"Run?" Bec snarled. "Run where? Think you can hide in Klittmann all your life? There won't be any Basement to go to after this."

Reeth was looking at Bec sardonically. "You really did it, didn't you? Thought you could take the whole city." He shook his head, smiled ruefully.

"Shut up!" Bec roared, and hit him across the face.

Reeth didn't seem perturbed or surprised. Bec was dialling on the vision phone, trying to get Bissey.

Eventually there came the hiss of the audio line but the paper screen remained a blank square of luminescence. This time Bissey wasn't showing himself.

"Yes?" a grunting, whispering voice said.

"What's the meaning of this, Bissey?" Bec demanded in hard tones. "This wasn't in the deal."

For answer there was only a dry laugh.

"I'll ruin your organics!" Bec fumed. "You won't get one pint of it back!"

"Stop kicking, little man," the dry husky voice said distantly from the vision phone. "Me, I'm just a small-time tank owner. But there are some pretty big boys up in the pile. They didn't like what you did. They wouldn't even let me go through with it, when they heard about it. They're making up the nutrient you stole. So enjoy yourself while you still got time."

The line went dead.

Bec brooded.

So did I. Bissey's whispering voice was still in my ears. It was an all too painful lesson in the power that resided in Klittmann, the power that Becmath had so badly underestimated.

The muffled explosions seemed to be getting louder and sharper. Shouts of consternation could be heard in the garages. Apparently the lid was cracking.

"I didn't see our sloop out there," Bec said at last. "Have you sent it out?"

"No, there didn't seem any point against the fleet out there," Reeth told him. "Anyway, we were waiting for you to get back."

"You did the right thing. Is it armed up and everything?"

"Yes. Ready to go."

"Put extra rations in. All we've got."

"Rations? What for?"

"*Do what I tell you*," Bec snapped. "Doesn't anything get through to you? After today our supply of everything is cut off."

Reeth went away to arrange things. Grale was still hovering around, nervous but tough.

"We're taking the sloop and making a break for it," Bec told him. "Just eight or nine of us. Tell the rest of the guys they'd better filter out through the back way while they can."

"Hell, why?" Grale said with a grin. "Let them klugs take what's coming. They'll help draw fire from us."

Bec gave him a hard look that meant business and then

turned to me. "We're taking the alchemist with us. Come and help me persuade him."

The laboratory was reached by a stairway in the corner of the garage where the sloop was kept. Reeth and a couple of others were throwing protein packs in its storage space as we went past. I admired its long black torpedo shape one last time, then we were clattering down the stairs.

Harmen seemed to be only vaguely aware of the events that were going on above his head. Usually he had half a dozen different experiments going, but this time there was only one. He sat at a table, making adjustments on a panel of dials. In the centre of the table was a big globular discharge tube — though he called them retorts, not discharge tubes — with at least half a dozen necks growing from it at the end of each of which was an electrode. Actually as I looked closer the retort was not globular at all, but was made up of a number of different cavities fitted together. Every few seconds the electrodes discharged in a rapid sequence with a loud *shuuush* and the globe flamed up. In the centre something was writhing and running through a spectrum of colours.

For a few moments we were captivated by the sight and didn't speak. With each *shuuuush* the writhing gas in the retort seemed to be taking a more definite shape. Then, for several fleeting seconds, it took on the firm, tiny form of a human being. The body was a gay reddish colour. It was bedecked in multi-coloured garments and it looked up at us, its arms spread towards us appealingly.

A shuddering gasp escaped me. Then the minuscule thing dissolved again into a writhing, formless cloud of colour. Harmen turned to us with a smile.

"Merely a phantom, I'm afraid. But my first step towards the creation of the Androgyne. It is possible, by means of a recipe now lost, to grow real flesh and blood homunculi that are no bigger than what you have just seen. However, they require special environments and so cannot be let out of their glass bottles."

"Don't say that in front of Klein, you'll make him nervous," Bec warned him. "I've got bad news for you, Harmen." Briefly he explained the situation.

"It always comes to this," the alk said regretfully, pursing his lips. "Among the original migrants who came to Killibol were a large number of American and German gangsters. It is the only tradition that has survived all these centuries. Yet to leave all this. . . ." He indicated the workroom with an expansive wave of his arm.

Suddenly Bec's tone became urgent and he glanced at me worriedly as he spoke. "Remember what we were talking about the other day?" he said to Harmen. "You know — the location?"

"Yes?" Harmen's eyebrows rose.

"Well, bring whatever instruments would be useful. And maps."

"You intend . . . ?"

"No," Bec replied hurriedly. "It's just that we have to have all options open."

All this was mystifying to me, but I took no notice. I was too conscious of what was going on overhead. Harmen rooted around and filled our arms with apparatus. Himself he just carried a few books and scrolls.

The garage was all but deserted. Bec's gang had all fled except the few he had detailed to man the sloop. We piled in and took our places. Bec ordered Harmen to hide in the storage hold.

We piled into the main garage where the lid was thumping and shaking under the impact of Hacker shells. It had held up pretty well; but now it was disintegrating. In places we could see the light coming in from outside.

"Right, just hold it," Bec said. "Let's hope she'll still move."

He got out of the sloop and made for the lid switch. At that moment there was a cry from behind us. Tone the Taker came staggering out of a doorway, clutching a box to his chest.

"Take me with you!" he yelled desperately. "Don't leave me here!"

Bec shrugged and gestured with his thumb for Tone to board. Then he pulled the switch. There was a heavy whine of motors.

The lid was beginning to lift when he scrambled back

breathlessly into the driving seat. The sloop surged forward, straight for the mass of steel and concrete.

Our acceleration, of course was terrific. The lid grumbled up then stuck with just enough clearance. In what seemed like the blink of an eyelid we were in the forecourt and among the cops.

They sure were surprised by our appearance. They didn't know about the sloop, and it was better than anything they had. Our big Hacker guns barked destruction as we raced past. Then we were streaking down the main thoroughfare, heading for the Southside ramp and the First Level Ring Road.

At that point I began wondering what Bec's destination was, where he intended to go and what he intended to do. Our only asset was the sloop; apart from that we were at the end of the road.

We made an entire circuit of the Ring Road at high speed, occasionally knocking aside other vehicles by sheer momentum, before the cops latched on to us again.

An explosion rocked the sloop. Bec wheeled us about, sped off the Ring Road into a narrower street where we were less exposed. Three cop-ships were on our tail.

I have to say this for Bec, his driving was terrific. I never knew the cops had as many sloops as they turned on us that day. We accounted for four, I think. Bec threw us up and down streets almost too narrow for us to go, and his judgment never faltered.

But the cops were cute too. They were edging us towards where they wanted us to go: the rim of the city. I know now that Bec accepted this with a kind of resignation; he had nowhere else to go.

Smoke was filling the inside of the sloop from all the firing we had been doing. The sloop slowed down, the motors idling. Suddenly I realised with a start that we were on the edge of a great empty concourse which ended in a great locked valve-like portal thirty feet in diameter.

We were near Klittmann's one and only exit.

Four or five police vehicles were parked in a ragged line some hundreds of feet away, keeping a respectful distance. To my surprise a cop stepped out and put a loud-hailer to his mouth.

His words floated towards us, faint and distorted.

"This city doesn't want you, Becmath. There's no place for you here. . . ."

Now the sloop had stopped. We all looked at Becmath, wondering what was happening. Then our eyes left him. Something was happening. The great lid of the exit valve was sliding smoothly up. Through the gaping circle we could see *landscape — outside*: dim, grey, cold.

The initial glimpse of that is an unforgettable experience to a Killibol city-man. For an Earthman, it would be like looking down a vast gaping chasm that has no bottom.

"You *knew*," I said accusingly to Bec. "You knew all the time."

"No!" Grale shouted. "Fight it out! Go down fighting!"

I don't think Bec heard either of us. A shell exploded nearby. He put the sloop in motion. We gathered speed, heading inexorably for the portal. Had the cops herded us here, I wondered, or had Bec lured them here? We lunged over the slight rise in the ground and sped through the great circle. Out. Into the dimness. The cold. The bare, dead rock.

And that was how we came to be expelled from Klittmann.

Four

Outside the light is always a little dimmer than we keep it in Klittmann, but our eyes quickly grew accustomed to it. On that first day, however, we kept the sloop's lights burning. The sun was sinking in the sky.

Day and night on Killibol go through a cycle of fifteen hours. When darkness fell Becmath kept on driving, seeing his way by means of headlights. Me, I settled down to sleep. When I woke the sun was up again and Bec was still driving. The alk was in the seat next to him, a map spread out on the dashboard. He was consulting a funny little instrument with a wavering needle.

Reeth handed me a slab of protein. I bit into it and enjoyed the fruity flavour. But it was soon gone and not much of a breakfast. While I ate I weighed up the bunch I was stuck with for good or ill.

Excluding Harmen and Tone the Taker, the four of us were part of the inner circle Becmath kept around him. There was Grale: flashy and boorish. He had a knack of being the first to move and of winding up with the biggest piece. I had a bad relationship with him. Then there was Hassmann, a big, bull-like type, not too bright but dependable if there wasn't much thinking to be done. He was the kind who never questioned an order but got on with the job.

Brightest of the three was Reeth. I got along with him best. He was what I call a reasonable guy.

They were all slum-bred, hard, and they could be cruel. But they were capable, and if a thing could be done they could do it. All the more so because they were schooled in Becmath's special kind of leadership and organisation. In a word, they were smart and knew a lot. In any tight spot they were the people I would choose to have with me. If there was any crack in this ruthless world where we could crawl, they were the guys to take advantage of it. The trouble was I didn't believe there was a crack.

Coming to Bec, he was smarter than them all, smarter than anybody. Among normal men Bec was sharp like a knife. I don't think any of us even felt resentful about his dragging us with him in his downfall. Big men make big mistakes.

I swallowed the last of the protein. "O.K.," I heard Bec say to the alk, "we'll keep going till we hit the river."

At that moment he apparently saw something through the window because he swerved sharply and slowed down to a crawl.

My pulse quickened when I took a look. There was a girl out there, walking along alone. When she saw us she ran. Bec drew alongside her and we shouted out to her, calling her names. I could hear her panting as she tried to get away.

"It's a nomad girl!" Bec said in excitement.

"Hey, pretty thing, you," Grale called, pulling down a window. "Come on, don't be coy."

"Fetch her in, boys." Bec pulled up to a stop.

A couple of the boys jumped out and grabbed her. They dragged her into the sloop and held her against the side panelling.

She glared at us hotly, defiantly. She wasn't wearing much, just a tattered gown that left one leg and one breast bare. When she moved it showed even more. Nomad girls have no sense of modesty, so I'd heard.

"Hey, she's good looking," Bec gloated. "Now listen, girl, with you out here on your own, and on foot too, your people can't be far away. Probably on the other side of that hill, right?"

She didn't answer.

"Let me take her in the back," I urged. "I'll screw it out of her."

Bec chuckled, half frowning. "That wouldn't scare a nomad girl. First things first, Klein, plenty of time for that later."

Suddenly she spoke. "Yeah, over the hill. Just right over."

"You'd better be telling me the truth, now." Bec wiped his mouth, looking speculatively at the low ground on the mid-horizon. "Listen, honey, we're going over the hill, and you'll show me which are the protein vans. Get it? You won't get hurt. If we grab one," he explained unnecessarily, "we can eat for good."

Motors whining, we crept up the hill, pausing on the crest. The girl pointed and giggled. "There!"

The nomad camp was down below sure enough. But we didn't linger for long. There was too much of it. Great vans and prime movers scattered about in the dust. And they spotted us almost as soon as we emerged over the rise. There was a puff as a mortar shell came whizzing our way.

Bec heaved on the wheel and we roared frantically down towards the plain. I shook the girl by the shoulders. "Pretty girl, you're taking a big risk by trying that on!"

"Well, boys," Becmath said sombrely, "that's what we can expect from nomad tribes, anybody big enough to have protein tanks. Banditry no good for us. O.K., we continue. We still got Plan A."

This was the first I'd heard of Plan A, but at that moment I had other things stirring me besides the threat of starvation. I dragged the nomad girl to the back of the driving cabin.

"What's your name, warm-belly?" I said, feeling her arms. "Gelbore."

"Well, Gelbore, you'll never see your people again."

She was scared and lost, but trying to put a good face on it. "So who worries?" she said brashly. She leaned against me, pressing into me gently.

"Maybe we'll starve. If so, you'll starve." Now I was fondling her uncovered breast. Perhaps it was the strangeness of the situation, but it made me feel dizzy, more dizzy than any woman ever had before.

Becmath spoke to me over his shoulder. "Don't get ideas, Klein. That woman cuts down our rations."

We were a good way from the nomad camp by now. Gelbore stared woefully out of the window, at the grey terrain and the receding hills.

"They're shifting out soon! If you drop me off I'll not walk back in time!"

"You're asking for favours. We haven't even got time to stop when we throw you off."

If you hit the ground at seventy miles per hour, I reckon your chances are something less than hopeful. Gelbore went limp in my arms when she heard this death sentence. Her head drooped.

"Hell, what difference does it make?" I objected. "If we die, we die, having her along won't change anything. Pity to waste her now we got her."

He was silent for some moments. Then he sighed, and shrugged. "You win. Stop worrying, little girl. For the time being anyway."

I took her back, past the motor housings, the magazine lockers, into the store hold. "It was *me* who fixed things for you," I murmured. She muttered words I didn't hear.

I stripped her robe off and it was really good, my hips grinding against hers. When it was over I found myself gazing at her face. For the first time I saw Gelbore as a person.

Becmath never seemed to need sleep. He insisted on driving the sloop himself most of the time, day and night. He would hand the wheel to myself, Reeth or Grale for a while, but four or five hours later he would be back and carry on sometimes for a twenty-hour stretch.

I was wondering what Tone would do when he ran out of pop. He had a store of it in the box he never let out of his sight, but it couldn't last for ever. Every so often he'd disappear into the back to give himself a shot. We never mentioned it, except Grale who used to taunt him sometimes.

It wasn't long before we all lost patience with Bec's silence. We wanted answers. Maybe we'd kept silence this far because of a hidden fear that there weren't any answers, that Bec had no ideas.

But life in the sloop was monotonous and we were starting to quarrel. More and more often Bec had to intervene to quieten us down. Eventually Reeth retorted: "Listen, boss, *we want to know where we're going.*"

"Feeling hungry, huh?" A hint of amusement came to Bec's face.

"You bet we're hungry," Hassmann complained. "What we're eating wouldn't keep a dog alive."

Bec nodded distantly, as if his thoughts were far away. "So

you want food. O.K., then listen to this. There's a place where food grows on the ground from horizon to horizon. When you walk you're treading it underfoot, you can't see the floor for everything that's growing there. Food just for the picking up. The name of that place is Earth."

Grale gave him a pained look. "Earth? Don't kid us on, boss, we're not stupid."

"I'll reserve an opinion on that. Get used to the idea, because Earth is where we're going."

"But that's impossible." This time it was Tone who spoke.

"I know what you're thinking," Bec answered. "Centuries ago the gateway from Earth was destroyed, blown up, its substance dispersed. The connection with Earth went with it and nobody has passed either way since. But there's something you don't know. Back in Klittmann I spent a lot of time talking to the alchemist. I'd call him the wisest man in Klittmann. He's studied all the old books and everything and he told me something about the gateway nobody else realises."

Harmen took all this praise impassively. The old coot, I thought, he's behind all this. He's captivated Bec with his weird theories.

"You may or may not know," Bec continued, "that the gate consisted of substance that existed both here on Killibol and simultaneously on Earth. What I for one didn't know was that the gateway was opened in the first place by an alchemist. That right, Harmen? Go on, tell them."

The alk nodded soberly. "True it is, as can be read in the ancient documents by one able enough to read the arcane symbols. The substance of the gateway was derived from *tincture*, the *prima materia* of existence which is not governed by the laws of space and time. Else how was the gateway possible — how could exoteric science have created something that existed in two locations at the same time? Tincture is indestructible, indivisible, and hence—" He broke off. "Let your leader tell you."

"It's certainly not in any of the workmen's manuals," Reeth admitted, rubbing his chin. "To tell the truth I've never given a thought in my life to how the gateway worked. That was all in the past, long before I was born."

"What Harmen means is," Bec resumed, "that though the

stuff the gateway was made of was scattered over hundreds of thousands of miles by an atomic explosion, it never really lost its cohesion. Over the centuries it sort of gathered itself up again, attracted to itself, as it were. And what's more, in the same place it was before. Harmen calculates that by now the gateway is reconstituted again."

Reeth was frowning. "You mean the molecules have all gravitated back to where they were before the explosion?"

"That's right," Bec began, but the alk corrected him. "Tincture has no molecules. Atomic and molecular matter are corruptions of the primordial *hyle*, which is single, whole and indivisible, yet not in a way that we can readily understand. To the gross senses it may seem possible for it to be divided in certain conditions. Then again, very great force can cause it to become attenuated to the point where it apparently vanishes; yet given time it reverts to the form given to it when it was first distilled. Hylic objects cannot be made to change their shape except by very difficult alchemical processes."

"And this is what will have happened to the gateway?" I queried.

"The gateway is not pure *hyle,* it is true; but the derivation is close enough for the same to hold."

"Well, there you have it, boys," Bec finished. "Don't worry if you don't understand all those technicalities. The important thing is that *we know where the gateway is.* And we should be able to reach it before our food runs out."

Grale had been cleaning his gun. He threw it down in an expression of disgust, a rare show of rebellion for him. "The whole thing is cock-eyed crazy! You know what I think, boss? We're being taken by an alk loon!"

"Oh, I don't know," Reeth said in calmer, meditative tones. "It sounds reasonable. I mean, it hangs together. But if you ask me it's an awful long shot."

"Sure, it's a long shot," Bec replied amiably. "It's a gamble. Maybe we'll never reach the gateway. Or maybe Harmen here is wrong about it. We'll soon know."

Grale was angry. "We should have stayed in Klittmann!"

"In Klittmann you'd be dead already. You think we had any choice about getting out? Wise up — we're all that's left of the organisation. In Klittmann we were the core, the main office, and the cops wouldn't have let up until they got us. I don't like this situation any more than you do."

Tone sniffed. His face had that sneaky, twitchy look that meant his system was crying out for a recharge. I knew what he was thinking. Whether there was any pop on Earth. Maybe he hoped that grew out of the ground there, too.

Bec resumed driving. I slid into the adjoining seat.

"What's it going to be like on Earth, boss?"

"There's no knowing. It seems Earth and Killibol exist at different . . . time-rates from one another." Plainly he had difficulty with the concept. "Sometimes one speeds up relative to the other, sometimes slows down. While centuries have passed here on Killibol something like a million years or more have gone by on Earth. It's anybody's guess what we'll find."

I let that sink in for a minute. "So it's a one-way trip. There's no coming back because. . . ."

Bec glanced at me fiercely. "Klein, we're coming back! Don't ever doubt that!" Suddenly he chuckled. "Confusing, isn't it? Think about it. If we spent a year on Earth and came back here, we'd find that only seconds had passed on Killibol. Actually it isn't even that complicated. Harmen says the two planets are currently synchronised in their time-rates. He says they're both at the apogee of their cycles. So if everything goes right — and I only give us fifty-fifty — we'll be able to pass to and fro at will between Earth and the Dark World."

"The Dark World?"

"Sure. That's what the old books call Killibol."

"Why?"

"I don't know. Of course, it's never very bright out in the open here. Not as bright as in the cities."

"It's not what you'd call dark, either."

"That's right." He was silent for a moment. Then he lifted his eyes upwards. There were stars in the sky. I'd watched them often in the last few days.

"You know something, Klein? Earth is in another galaxy. Billions of light-years away. Just think of it! It's an awful long way away."

A day later Bec brought the sloop to a halt for a few minutes. The engines ticked over in the midst of the same sombre, grey plains. In the middle distance stood a city.

"According to the map that's Chombrel," Bec said. "It's a dead city now. Their tanks caught a plague."

He circled it slowly, studying it. Something about it seemed to interest him. And in fact it didn't look like Klittmann. It was more sculptured. Its walls rose straighter, but then broke off jaggedly.

"Chombrel was architecturally fashioned to represent a dead tree stump," Bec said finally. "See the way it juts up on one side, as if the trunk had broken off?"

I'd seen a picture of a tree once, but the whole thing meant little to me. Bec put the sloop on course again. "It's a queer, involved kind of symbolism on a dead world. . . ."

What else he might have said I don't know, because just then I noticed something I didn't like. Grale had Gelbore up against the rear wall of the cabin. By now she thought of herself as my girl, and so did I. She was too scared to resist, but she glanced at me, perplexed and distressed.

I shot across the cabin and jerked him away. Coolly he checked me, holding up his hand threateningly, dangerously.

"Hold it, man. A woman is everybody's property."

Bec looked at us, then turned back to the wheel. "What's the matter with you, Klein? This isn't too considerate."

Hotly Gelbore and I exchanged feelings through the eyes. "The girl is mine!" I snarled. "Any klug who wants her passes me first."

Becmath still did not deign to present more than his back to the argument, but he said sternly: "Now listen, *you klugs.* Any trouble over our little nomad girl and I myself will throw her off the sloop. So calm it."

Grale had a slack-mouth grin. "And who gets the girl?"

"Klein is over you. Do what he says."

It didn't make me feel good that Bec had to reassert my authority over the others like that; but at least I had Gelbore. Grale gave me a dirty look and then joined Reeth, Hassmann and Tone in a game of cards. Gelbore huddled with me in a corner, regarding them with fear.

"Don't worry," I murmured. "They had it hard enough in Klittmann not to hold any resentment. You just stick with me."

"Sure, I'll stick with you," she murmured back, giving a little shiver.

I left her and dropped back into the seat next to Bec. "Thanks," I said.

"Don't thank me," he replied harshly. His voice was hard and brutal, harder than I had ever heard it before.

Eventually we came to a broad river of clear water, which according to Harmen's map we had to cross. Floating down the river were big slabs of the lighter-than-water rock that is found in some parts. When the stream proved too deep for the sloop to ford, Reeth proposed that we lash it to one of these slabs.

The job took some time, but everyone brought up in Klittmann is something of a mechanic — as well as an electrician and builder. We managed to grapple one of the bigger slabs and hauled it to the shore using the sloop's engine. The hardest part was lashing the sloop down safely. Then we cast off and went flowing downstream.

There was a landmark we had to watch for, so Bec figured we might as well stay on the water until we found it. The rock slab was bigger in area than the sloop, and we took to sitting out on it, detailing a couple of men at a time to steer us with poles.

I found myself sitting with Bec, alone and out of earshot of the others. Bec was eager to talk about those things difficult to understand that were so typical of him of late. When he looked at the others his expression was sardonic and he gave a half-grunt, half-chuckle.

"Gangsters," he said. "That's what we are, gangsters. Remember what the alchemist said? Gangsters loomed large among the people who came to Killibol. Maybe the corruption and stagnation began with that. But you know something, Klein? *We* are gangsters, and we are sharper than anybody in Klittmann."

"That may be so," I replied, "but here we are outside."

"Yeah, that's right. You know why? Only we represent *change* in Klittmann. We are dangerous. Have to be eliminated. Listen to me, Klein: we could be the germ of something different on this world. Yes, gangsters and all. Who else is there?

In Klittmann now there is only self-interest. We could go beyond that — make a state that existed for itself and commanded the allegiance of all men. A state that conquered other cities and made an empire that released inventiveness in men and changed the whole world."

I guess Bec had been working on me for a long time. Ever since I had met him, if the truth were known, I had been coming under the spell of his personality and of his ideas. Some of them I didn't understand, but he had aroused a kind of loyalty in me that was like something magical. Certainly it went far beyond my upbringing.

"That state, that empire," he told me, "is the hope of mankind. Something not for a man's own sake, but for the sake of the thing itself. You with me Klein?"

"Why are you telling me this?" I asked, swallowing.

"The others are good guys — capable. But that's all. Reeth maybe . . . but Grale and Hassmann? Not on your life. They're mindless klugs. Tools. *You* have a mind, Klein. Maybe it's pretty hard to find sometimes . . . but I've watched you. An idea gets through to you in the end.

"So my state, Klein, that comes before everything else. A city that progresses, right?"

I was carried away by what he was saying. It seemed to me that here was the first new, clean thing I had heard since I was born. A sense of loyalty that went beyond all personal considerations; here was what Bec was putting to me, and it sounded invincible. Maybe that's ridiculous considering the situation we were in, but Bec had that quality: he could make even defeat seem fascinating and hopeful.

"Before everything, right?" Bec repeated. "Even before a woman."

Gelbore was sitting on the edge of the raft, trailing her hand in the water. I looked at her and swallowed again. Much though I was inspired by Bec's vision, there was one thing I had to admit.

"Sometimes nothing comes before a woman, Bec," I said.

So what did Becmath do when he heard this?

He took out his handgun and before I fully realised what was happening he shot Gelbore. From former occasions I was familiar with the accuracy of Bec's shooting. She took it in the head. Without a single cry she toppled into the water and disappeared from view.

When I saw her falling off the raft like a lump of clay my guts knotted into a tight ball. At the same time something indescribably sweet and painful passed through me. I sprang to my feet, on fire.

"You klug! I'll kill you for that!"

"The state first, Klein." Bec's voice was incongruously gentle.

A man has to be logical. "O.K.," I pledged with difficulty. "The state first."

From that moment Bec had me hooked in a condition of unshakable loyalty. It was the first time in my life I had known real dedication. I think I had to have that, or I would never have been able to face the fact that I did nothing to avenge the killing of Gelbore.

And yet the whole thing was insane. Here we were, practically dead men, while Bec spouted dreams about state and empire. He talked to me more during the journey, expanding on his plans. He would establish regular traffic between the cities, he said, wipe out the nomad bands and set up staging posts so that travellers could replenish their supplies en route. It all sounded fine, the only missing part was how he was going to achieve all this.

But like I say, by now I was hooked on the dream and instead of greeting it with scepticism or derision I took it all with an air of hard-headed realism.

During the second day on the river we saw the landmark that would lead us to the gateway: a thousand-foot column of stainless steel. It was weathered and worn, corroded in places. Obviously it had been there a long time, but just as obviously it must have been erected after the nuclear explosion had destroyed the gateway. For some reason the people of that time had left it there as a marker.

Beyond the pillar a shallow valley ran between two long, rounded mounds for about two to three miles. After we grounded the sloop we followed it to where the mounds met. At the junction, or just before it, the ground was fissured into a gaping chasm that ran a fair distance. Situated neatly over that chasm was something that at first you weren't sure was there.

It was like a big transparent, very clear jelly with a lavender tint. In shape it was an elongated ovoid, a big egg.

Bec looked at the alchemist.

Harmen nodded. "My calculations were correct. That's it."

We all got out to explore. When you touched the material of the gateway it was like putting your hand in very thin water. Thin oil, maybe. It didn't impede motion but it felt cool and smooth.

The fissure was a couple of hundred feet deep. Its being there was probably accidental — accidental insofar as it was a by-product of the atomic explosion centuries ago — because the ground thereabouts was considerably broken up and smaller cracks rayed out at various angles.

We went back to the sloop to talk it over. "How do we know it still works?" Grale snapped tensely.

"Have you got any instrument that might test it?" Bec asked Harmen.

The alk shook his head. "Afraid not. The only way is to try it out. The gate is directional, by the way. You have to enter it from the right direction. Going through from this end of the egg, straight between the walls of the valley, will take you to Earth. You get nowhere by trying it from any other angle. Likewise you take the reverse procedure to get from Earth to Killibol."

Hassmann sighed. "And if it don't work you go to the bottom of the gulf. That's pretty!"

"You've played crazier games, Hassmann." Bec settled himself comfortably in the driver's seat and started the motors.

"You're not taking us through just like that!" Grale protested. He was sweating slightly. "We ought to send somebody through first! To see if it works! To see what's on the other side—"

"And if it doesn't work, Grale, what are you gonna do then? You want to sit here and starve?"

Bec twisted round to look Grale straight in the eyes as he said this. We were all silent.

Grale started to laugh.

Bec backed up the sloop to get a good run. Then we went

at the gateway full tilt. The Big Egg loomed up, shimmering
— suddenly Grale and Reeth let loose with Jain guns and gave
out raucous whoops and laughs to give vent to their nervous
energy—

There was an instant of utter darkness. Then we came out
into the sunlight — and man! We all knew why they call
Killibol the Dark World.

We had to wear eye-filters ever since. The sun seared my
eyes like a white-hot iron. The landscape had a million
colours which thrust themselves into my eyeballs like knives.

How bright it is! How bright is that place!

Five

Have you ever been in a reactor room when they let the shields down? It was like that. Light: blinding, dazzling light that came pouring through the sloop's windows. I got a split-second impression of incredible colours and then I could see nothing but glare and I flung my arms across my eyes, gasping with the pain that lanced through them.

All was confusion, with everybody yelling and going crazy. Hassmann fell heavily against me; Grale and Reeth continued firing the Jains, yelling their heads off, even though they were blind.

I knew we'd hit ground on the other side because the sloop bumped and rolled forward, jerking and swaying. Shortly it came to a stop, and I could hear Bec cursing violently, and screaming for silence.

"The shutters! The shutters, you klugs!"

His penetrating voice goaded me into action. I found a lever that brought down a section of the steel shutters that could seal all the windows, afterwards closing the eye-holes. Bec was stumbling about the sloop, grabbing anybody he found and pulling levers. He pulled Grale and Reeth away from their clattering Jains, at which they protested loudly.

Gradually things quietened down. All the shutters were in place and we were in pitch blackness.

Bec switched on the inside lights. We sat staring at one another inside our steel cocoon, sweating and trying to get back the use of our sight.

What was out there? What had we dropped in the middle of? Grale jumped up again and made for one of the Hackers. Bec pushed him back down.

"You think we got all the ammunition in the world?"

"We're sitting here blind doing nothing!" Grale near-screamed. "Anything could be out there — we could be wiped out!"

"SHUT UP!" Bec bellowed.

It was like Grale to get hysterical when he was scared, but in this case he was speaking for all of us. We were all scared — scared of the unknown, or what might lie on the other side of the sloop's armoured hull. Even Bec, I could see, was far from calm.

"Nothing's happened yet, has it?" he snapped. He glared at each of us in turn. "You punks handled that like a bunch of knock-kneed virgins."

There was a long pause.

"In the old days they called Killibol the Dark World," Bec said at last. "That's right, isn't it, Harmen? Maybe they called it that because Earth is so bright."

Harmen was squatting in a corner, electing himself out of the proceedings as usual. "Undoubtedly," he replied in a sonorous voice. "It would appear that the light here is so bright as to be unbearable to us. Over the centuries our eyes have presumably become accustomed to Killibol's dimness."

"Then we're as good as blind," Reeth said.

"Naw." Bec waved his hand. Harmen rose and disappeared muttering into the storage hold. He returned with a pair of dark goggles I had last seen on his workbench back home.

"Brilliant light is a frequent by-product of alchemical operations," he said. "These filters provide adequate protection."

He began to fit the goggles over his lined brow. "Open the shutter and let me view the world of our forebears," he ordered imperiously.

"Here, gimme those." Bec charged over and snatched the goggles from him. Quickly he adjusted them to his own head. "Better hide your eyes, boys. I'm going to take a look."

We obeyed. I heard a shutter open. There was silence for some moments. Then Bec grunted.

"Come over here, Klein," he said.

I groped my way forward and met Bec's outstretched arm. He handed the goggles to me. I put them on, pulling the headband tight. Cautiously I opened my eyes and stared out of the window, ignoring Bec's turned back.

So there it was. All the fears my imagination had invented, like our having fallen into a furnace, melted away.

The light was so strong that it warmed my skin, a sensation that I found oddly pleasant. A peaceful landscape stretched out before me. Instead of the flat, grey expanse of rock I had been staring at for the past twenty days or so, I saw a terrain that, though flat hereabouts, broke up into undulating hills in the mid-distance and was covered with a carpet of a green growth that at first I thought was some sort of plastic or artificial fibre. Then I told myself that it couldn't be, and I felt a sense of excitement as I realised what the green growth was.

Further off I saw a clump of column-like structures crowned with masses that moved slightly. They had to be trees, I thought to myself after a while.

Even when wearing the goggles the light was unnaturally brilliant and enhanced the scene with an eerie, dream-like quality. Overhead, the sky was a vivid blue and was studded with clouds of white water-vapour.

I took a careful look at it all, then closed the shutter and removed the goggles. I turned to face the others. Bec was grinning.

"The panic's over," I said. "There's nothing moving out there. We're alone."

"What's it like?" Hassmann asked eagerly. "Is there food?"

"There's food," Bec announced proudly. "It's like I said it would be. Organics growing underfoot."

Grale began grumbling again. "That's just fine. But how do we see to pick it up?"

Bec looked at Harmen. "Have you got any more of these goggles? Or can you make any?"

"I think so," the alk said. "I believe we have the requisite materials."

Reeth and myself helped Harmen make the light-filters. It didn't take long. In the hold was a sheet of dark-coloured barely-transparent material which we cut into strips and fastened into rims of foam plastic, fastening on headbands. In an hour we had a set for everybody, even Tone the Taker.

The guys were all nervous and expectant as Bec let up the shutters.

For a long time they sat staring at the scenery.

Then Bec opened the sloop's big door.

"Come on, you guys, you're not paralysed," he complained. "Get down and tread the new world."

We were all reluctant to move. We felt safe inside the sloop. Exasperated, Bec started grabbing at us and shoving us through the door. Grale picked up a repeater before he would go. Breezes tugged at our skin as we climbed to the ground, and we felt awkward and uneasy in the newly-made goggles. In an instinctive gesture of protection we stood with our backs to the sloop and gazed about us.

"It's *weird*," Reeth murmured.

The Big Egg loomed faintly some distance off, the sloop having rolled nearly two miles before it stopped. I had to look hard to see it at all; it was much less noticeable than on Killibol and was no more than a patch of mist in the air. If you didn't know where to look you'd never find it at all.

The green growth was spongy underfoot. Skywards, the sun, although it was much smaller than the big, pale Killibol sun, was still too bright to look at directly, even with the goggles. Also in the sky was another, much larger body: a huge yellow globe covered with various darker markings. Another planet, hanging close to Earth in space.

Tone the Taker had noticed it, too, and was staring upwards with rapt attention.

"Beautiful," he murmured. "Like a pop dream."

None of the others, Harmen possibly excepted, had the equipment to see anything artistic in the scene. To them it was just fact, as the streets and buttresses of Klittmann were facts. True, as I looked longer at the eerie, strangely *living* landscape I felt a yearning for that vast towering pile of stone, steel and concrete; for falling dust, for dives and joints and the incessant babble of clipped Klittmann speech. But I knew none of us were going to crack up over it. We'd already gone through all our traumas that day we fled through Klittmann's portal.

Suddenly I jerked as Grale raised his repeater and yanked back the trigger. The gun juddered continuously until he had emptied a whole clip into thin air, sending it spraying out all over the empty landscape.

He turned back to us grinning, mouth slack, eyes hidden behind the dark goggles.

"Feel better?" Bec asked acidly.

"Sure. Just making myself at home. I like to feel I can lick this place."

Bec grimaced and turned to the rest of us. "Well, boys, we made it. Here it is. No bare rock anywhere. Protein just waiting to be picked up. *Food.*"

Dumbly we stared at the ground. The green carpet of organics was the hardest thing to get used to. People from Killibol have a reverence for organics and we didn't know where to put our feet.

Hassmann was the first to try it (sometimes it's an advantage not to be hampered by an over-active imagination). Wonderingly he knelt on one knee and pulled up a handful of the green stuff that grew in long, thin blades. Later Harmen found from a book that the old Earth word for it was *grass*. Hassmann sniffed it, ran it between his fingers, then reluctantly put some of it in his mouth. He chewed for nearly a minute, making a sourer face all the while, until he finally spat it out.

"It don't taste good, boss. We've got a bum steer."

Bec cropped some of the grass himself, feeling it and tasting it. He looked questioningly at Harmen. The alchemist shook his head.

"I know nothing of Earth food."

Doubtfully Bec looked towards the trees. "O.K.," he decided after a while, "maybe you have to look around for the right stuff. But there's food here all right. Everybody knows that."

We were all glad to get back aboard the sloop. An air of indecision had suddenly come over the gang. We all felt reluctant to move away from the gateway. Bec realised he had to squash this feeling right away.

He put the sloop in motion, talking to us as he drove. "Planet Earth is a big place, boys. It might take us a while to case this joint. Meanwhile keep your eyes open but don't get nervy. Get used to the eye-shades because you're going to be wearing them for a long, long time. And don't get trigger-happy because we've only got so much ammunition and we'll probably need it. This sloop is our ace card, boys, just like it was in Klittmann. So don't shoot without an order — hear that, Grale?"

Grale grunted.

But it was Hassmann who forgot Bec's instruction and let out a long panicky burst on the Jain he was nursing before we'd gone three miles. Bec pulled up fast and turned to face us furiously.

"What did I just say to you?" he stormed, his eyes blazing.

We all looked at the landscape. There was nothing there.

"Something was coming at us, boss!" Hassmann objected. "A bomb or a missile. I had to shoot! Look, there it is right out there!" He pointed to the black object he had expertly shot down, lying in the grass.

In the end it was Reeth who ventured out to inspect it. He brought it back for us to see: it was a flying animal. He spread out the feathered wings. Blood dripped on to the floor from where the Jain bullets had hit it.

"Say, look up there," Grale said. A mate to the dead bird was soaring over us, wheeling with wings outspread.

"I don't get it," Grale said, puzzled. "How does it stay up?" Flying animals, and flying machines, were unknown on Killibol.

Wordlessly Bec went back to the driving seat. We saw more birds after that.

As we travelled Bec drew a map, using surrounding hills as landmarks so we could always find our way back to the gateway again. The sloop rolled bumpily over the uneven turf, clambering awkwardly up and down slopes, but the Earth day is considerably longer than the Killibol day and we covered about a hundred miles per rotation period. During the night we could dispense with our eye-shades; but Bec insisted on travelling by day so as to acclimatise ourselves. He also insisted on everybody getting out of the sloop at each stop we made; otherwise most of us would have been happier huddling in our own artificial little world.

We passed through grassland, past forest, lakes and rivers. We spent some time arguing whether animals as well as plants might constitute food. So far we had found nothing that we could regard as even remotely eatable. On one of our stops Hassmann entered a forest and shot a small animal he found there, after hearing Harmen and Reeth both assert that animal tissue contains more protein than does vegetable tissue.

Actually the food we were used to always came in processed slabs or cakes differing only in flavour and texture. That was why we didn't think of the idea of eating flesh straight away. Hassmann peeled off the creature's fur and cut a piece off it with a hacksaw. Blood was running all over his hands and on to the ground where we sat in the shadow of the sloop. He sniffed at the chunk of meat, which was red and soggy.

My gorge rose. We all shook our heads. Disgusted, Hassmann flung the dead animal away with all his strength and wiped his hands on the grass.

"Like trying to eat your own arm!"

Grale swallowed the last of his protein bar. The rations were low: none of us had had a full belly for a long time.

He stood up and moved around restlessly. "I'll bet there's nothing to eat on the whole of this Goddamned planet. We should have stayed in Klittmann and died fighting."

Bec stared at him with interest. "I never knew a guy so unhappy to be alive."

"What's the good of being alive walking around like a crazy alk?" He tapped his eye-shades. "When are we gonna find what we came for?"

"He's got something there, boss," Reeth put in mildly. "It don't look good."

"It don't look good to you because you can't see any further than the end of a gun barrel." Bec's voice was heavy with sarcasm. "You want it all handed to you. Sure I don't know what we're going to find, or when. I do know that whatever it is, we've got to be ready to handle it. If we don't find food we'll find people. Where there's people there are angles — and then there'll be food. You'll see Klittmann again: we'll break it open like a mud pie and drown the bosses in their own tanks."

Grale's florid face became dangerous. "What are you trying to pull, Bec?" he raged. "There's five of us! We've got no mob to back us up. We're finished, washed out! *How* are we gonna take Klittmann, Bec? *How?*"

"Quit squalling like a kid and shut up."

Grale stormed into the sloop to clean his guns, which he always did when he was feeling moody.

Everybody avoided saying anything. Even Harmen looked pensive.

Later Bec sent Reeth and me to climb a hill to spy out the land. All we saw of interest was a lake glinting in the distance. I stood there on top of the hill, under an open blue sky, trying not to feel naked and vulnerable (even now I still can't stand under an open sky without feeling naked) and trying not to think of close-packed, grey Klittmann where everything was machinery, artificial and familiar.

"Tell me," Reeth said in a dry, matter-of-fact voice, looking into the distance, "do you think Bec's cracking up?"

"Why should he be?"

"Well, he talks about going back to Klittmann. About taking it over as if nothing had happened. Grale's right — we've been knocked out of the game. Bec's ravings don't make sense."

I glanced thoughtfully at Reeth's narrow, sharp face. He had buck teeth that puckered up his features and made him appear shrewd, which he was. He was also nimble-minded and cool-headed. I could never understand why Bec had always ranked him below Grale.

"What I mean is," Reeth went on calmly, "I would feel like some kind of dummy following a guy who's flipped in the head."

"That sounds reasonable," I said, "but I don't think you need worry. I think Bec was getting interested in Earth a long time before we got hit. Ever since he met Harmen. He always seemed to reckon we would find something useful there."

Reeth gave an open-handed gesture, shrugging hopelessly. "But let's face it. We're mobsters. We're way out of our element here. Bec talks as if we're going to find cities here just the same as on Killibol. We're not. It's all different here."

"Bec has a theory about that," I told him confidentially. "He banks on there being a civilisation here. Where there's a civilisation there has to be mobsters. Once we contact them we can learn how they operate, what the angles are. Then we move in."

Simple. It takes a genius like Bec to see things that simple.

Reeth snorted delightedly. "And what if these other mobsters don't like us, if they wipe us out?"

"Bec has an angle there too," I said, grinning ruefully. "I

hope he's right. He reckons we should be smarter than they are. Life here on Earth is a lot easier than where we come from. In Klittmann we were struggling for survival since we were born. It's a law of evolution that we'll be better in the survival business than they are."

"Well, maybe," Reeth sighed. "It all sounds pretty theoretical to me. I trust facts, not theories."

"You can trust Bec. Who else could have got us out of that jam in Klittmann?"

"Who else could have got us *into* that jam? Klein, I'm wondering what will happen if we don't find any food. How long will this mob hang together if we don't find some action soon? If you ask me Bec's dipping into a pack and hoping to draw a card that isn't even there."

He sighed and indicated the stretching prairie. "I don't understand why we can't eat this stuff."

"Maybe it's like raw protein straight out of the tank," I surmised. "It could be that it has to be processed."

"But that needs factories and skilled technicians. If life's like that on Earth too then we've got it all wrong."

Regardless of my secret oath of loyalty to Bec, I couldn't think of an answer.

We went back down the hill to report. Hassman, Grale and Bec were playing cards. Tone the Taker sat skulking by himself some yards away. He had a miserable existence on the sloop; none of the mob deigned to notice him, apart from Bec, and Bec was too busy to bother with him. Now he sat clutching his box of pop, which he almost never put down. He was trying hard to ration himself, but the supply was dwindling day by day and his situation was pretty desperate. Lately his twitches had become more pronounced, which made the others despise him all the more despite that their fortunes in Klittmann had been partly founded on pop.

Only Harmen treated him like a human being, and now the alk also sat by himself, apparently contemplating.

As the sun went down everybody disappeared one by one into the sloop to get some sleep, until I was alone with Bec again. I told him about Reeth's misgivings, and added my own for good measure.

Bec was just finishing a tube of weed. He threw the stub down.

He said: "When a bullet is fired from a gun, sometimes it hits its target, and sometimes it misses. Whether it hits or not, it carries the same force. It can't do anything else. I'm that bullet."

"So that's all there is to it," I said dully. "We missed."

"Not at all. I'm a bullet with a name written on it. You know the old saying: sooner or later the bullet's going to hit the guy with that name. In other words, I've got a destination. Maybe it looks hopeless to you. But not to me, or to Harmen either."

"Harmen?"

Bec smiled. "You ought to talk to Harmen some time, Klein. He's got quite an outlook. I get inspiration from listening to him. He makes everything sound like a big machine that just has to keep on working. And the laws of the machine are the same on Killibol, on Earth, or anywhere in the universe."

"All right," I said with a shrug, "so what?"

"So if a thing will work in one place it will work in another. Take the lever: the principle of the lever is the same everywhere. You need a load, a fulcrum, and a force. You boys, yourself, Grale, Reeth and Hassmann, are my lever. I'm the force. Together we make up a machine, a lever that moved things for us back there in Klittmann. So why shouldn't it move things for us in the same way here? It will, once we find the right angle. We need a load to move and the right fulcrum. Then we have *power*."

I shook my head. "It's a little too abstract for me."

I decided to change the subject.

"You're going to have trouble with Grale, Bec. He's getting wild."

Bec laughed shortly. "Grale's a good man. He's dependable. But for you, he'd be my second. That puzzles you, doesn't it?"

"Yes," I admitted sourly.

He laughed again. "I grant you Reeth is smarter, but then he's got that individualistic streak. He's always liable to take off on his own. Grale is always shooting off his big mouth, but he sticks with it every time."

"Doesn't it bother you that we hate one another's guts?"

"No, it doesn't. It keeps you both on your toes." My resentment seemed to amuse him. "You've still got a few things to learn about leadership, Klein."

Maybe I had. There was still something left to learn about Becmath, too.

On the seventh day we found the village.

Six

Scents. That was the first thing I noticed as we poised on the breast of the hill overlooking the village. A mingle of scents drifting in through the sloop's windows.

Killibol people have a dulled sense of smell (only much later did I learn what a sharp, musty odour Klittmann has) and mine was awakening gradually. I remember that instance above the village as a small moment of truth.

The hill descended in a series of terraces to a cluster of buildings with quaint curved roofs; they appeared to be arranged in streets. The scents were breezing up from slender trees and giant trumpet-shaped flowers that grew on the terraces and had the appearance of being cultivated.

There was music drifting up the hillside, too. It was cordial and relaxed and made you think of beautiful things — quite unlike the jerky, frenetic music of Klittmann.

Bec beckoned Harmen to sit with him. "What do you think?"

We peered at the figures that were moving about the village. "It looks peaceful," the alk said. "Make friendly contact."

Bec nodded and began to lower us carefully down the hillside. The buildings grew larger as the sloop groaned downwards terrace by terrace.

When we were about halfway something whanged in through the window and ricocheted about inside. I yelled an order: in no time at all the shutters were down, closed to slits. A shower of tiny missiles rained against the hull with spitting sounds.

Reeth was peering through a slit. "There's a bunch of guys on the outskirts of the village shooting at us with guns of some kind."

"O.K.," Bec said instantly, "use one of the Hackers. Just a few shells."

"Is that wise?" I asked. "We don't know what these people have to back them up."

"We've got to show them we can fight, too," Bec said tightly. "The Hacker, Reeth."

Reeth obliged. Hacker shells landed amongst the firing party and in a brief shower around the village. As the shells exploded buildings collapsed in clouds of dust and all the inhabitants in sight scattered and vanished.

Bec flung us down the hill with engines whining, through terraced gardens which our wheels ripped to shreds. At the base of the hill the sloop's armoured prow smashed into the side of a house, bringing it crashing around us. Grumbling through the wreckage, the sloop pulled itself free and clambered over a further pile of rubble. Then we found ourselves in a wide street running the whole length of the village.

We slid slowly along it like a big black slug.

"What now?" I said. We all had triggers under our fingers but there was no one in sight.

"This time *they* can come to us," Bec announced. "Fire the Jains into the air. That might give them the idea."

Down here among the houses the noise of the Jains was deafening. After a short burst Bec ordered us to quit and we lay waiting in dead silence.

It took the villagers nearly an hour to make a move. Then, at the end of the street, two figures appeared and walked hesitantly towards us.

"This is where we find out who's on top," Bec mumbled. "Klein, come with me. The rest of you, keep us covered — and keep us covered *good*."

We opened the door, looked around, climbed down and went to meet the villagers where they were standing out in front of the sloop. I kept my hand on my gun. People who shoot without asking questions always make me nervous.

The Earth people were human beings, but obviously a different type of human from what we were. They had green skin: a light, gentle, pleasant green. Their eyes were a glowing purple.

They were slightly taller than us, but also more slender.

Their musculature was a little different, too: their faces were finely moulded and smooth-knit, firmer and more curved than our own faces. There was something delicate and sensitive about them.

Their clothes were highly coloured and flowed loosely when they walked. They glanced at the sloop, then back at us, then spoke in fluid tones.

"Pretty talk, eh, Klein?" Bec muttered out of the corner of his mouth. "A pity we can't follow it." He shook his head at the others.

They listened closely to his words, frowning. One of them pointed at him, then up at the big yellow planet in the sky. His face held a question.

"Whaddya think of that?" Bec said wonderingly. "They think we're from that big planet up there." Again he shook his head.

The Earthmen looked puzzled and confused. Bec, however, was satisfied.

"I think we hold the whip hand here for the moment," he said. "Let's install ourselves while we find out what goes on. One of these buildings should do — I don't know about you, but I'm getting pretty sick of the sloop."

Bec picked out a house and, using gestures, got the villagers to understand that he wanted to occupy it. With surprisingly little resistance they complied. The doors opened; more green-skinned people filed out, looking at us wide-eyed and curious.

There were kids among them, too. It didn't bother me too much that we might have killed some of those green-skinned children. I had a heady feeling knowing that we'd won the first round and that we could take anything we wanted.

Needless to say, the first thing we wanted was Earth protein.

Reeth moved up the sloop to cover the doorway of the building we had appropriated. We cased it inside. Bec kept one of the villagers with us (he turned out to be their head man) and sent the other with orders — if he had understood us right — to bring food.

I had to admit that the house was a very pleasant place. These people had a flair for design and colour. The house had five rooms, two of them above the others; the walls were of brick, stained in various pastel hues to create random patterns, and hung with drapes. Some of the walls were also padded with velvet.

Windows opened on to a garden at the back. We covered them up with the drapes so we could discard the goggles we were still wearing. We hung a lot of drapes in front of the door, too, so that we could get in and out without letting in too much light.

While we waited for the food to arrive I examined the furniture, which was hand-carved from a dark brown substance that had a good dry feel to it. All this was luxury such as I had never envisaged before. It even took a stretch of the imagination to realise that it *was* luxury. I'm sure Grale and Hassmann, Bec too, maybe, never even noticed it. I wondered briefly if the magnates and council members living up the pile in Klittmann had surroundings like this, but I quickly dismissed the idea. Their sensibilities, like mine, had been trained since birth to accept what was grey and leaden.

"Somebody's coming," Grale warned.

The drapes moved. I drew my gun. It had to be all right, though, because Reeth was still outside keeping guard in the sloop.

Three females entered and stood uncertainly in the dimmed room.

I knew straight away they were female. Their bodies swelled out in the right places. Their faces, too . . . they were even more sensitive-looking than the men, and alive in the way some women's faces are; softer, and fuller.

They were carrying bowls. The head man spoke to them and beckoned them to the table. They set the bowls down, making one place for each of us. He dismissed them, sat down, indicated our places for us, and began eating.

The smells coming from those bowls nearly knocked me out. I'd never smelled anything like it before: Killibol food doesn't give off any odour to speak of. Those smells were something so rich, so thick and overpowering, that they filled your nostrils and seemed to go right down into your inner being.

We sat down with the bowls before us. "Hey," hissed Reeth. "What if they're poisoning us? You know how easy it is to do — to turn out a batch of poison protein."

"Have no fear," rumbled the alk, holding the bowl in his

nands. "Natural tissues cannot be processed in that way." He took a deep breath, drawing in the fumes. "This indeed is alchemy!"

"Anyhow, he's eating it," I observed, looking at the Earthman.

We watched him to see what you were supposed to do. The food was hot and consisted of pieces of protein floating in a thick liquid. By the side were additional slabs of some fluffy stuff that in texture was a little like some of the protein slabs we were used to. He was picking up the solid pieces out of the bowl with his fingers and mopping up the liquid with the fluffy slabs.

So we ate, and in seconds were absolutely absorbed. The villagers could have walked in and slaughtered us all there and then without us even noticing. The flavours, though so strange, were so intense and penetrating, the feel of the food as it went down so utterly delicious, that it seemed to me it was better than anything I had ever known. Even better than sex. That first meal on Earth is something I'll remember all my life.

I learned afterwards that I was right — most Earth food did have to be processed. But the processing was fairly simple. The meal we ate consisted of plant and animal matter heated in water with various kinds of flavouring until its constituency changed by chemical action. That was the trick we would never have guessed.

When he had finished Bec leaned back, patting his stomach. "If we wanted we could go back to Killibol right now," he said, grinning. "We've already got a new racket. People would sell their mothers for food like this."

We stayed for quite a time in the village. It was called Hesha. Life there was easy and pleasant — eventually even their females got to look good to us, after we had acclimatised ourselves to our surroundings.

Bec sewed the village up with his usual efficiency. He made a small fortress of our headquarters, unbolting a couple of Jains from the sloop and positioning them at the front and the back of the house. Then he put the sloop back up on the hill overlooking the village where it commanded everything and in addition provided a good look-out for anyone else who might be arriving. I'd been real glad not to have to live in the sloop any more — it fairly stank of us by now — but Bec instituted a roster by which I and Reeth alternated with Grale and Hassmann, spending two days in the sloop and two days down below. It wasn't too bad, though.

Meantime Bec wanted to find out everything. He made us all learn the local language — even Grale, who at first exploded at the suggestion with the words, "Let the klugs learn Klittmann!" Within a few months we all had a working knowledge. Bec and Harmen were experts.

The green people called their country Rheatt. The village Hesha lay a fair way out from their main centres of population, and in time it became evident that no one would be arriving to relieve them from our occupation. They didn't exactly welcome our presence, of course, but they were much less against it than you might have imagined: because they feared their other enemy, the enemy for whom we had been mistaken, much more.

Rheatt was being invaded by Merame, the planet in the sky. Harmen had other names for it: Moon, Luna, and Selena. It orbited Earth at a distance of about eighty thousand miles, and he nation living there had spaceships which could make the journey quite easily. According to Harmen's books it should have been much further away, more like a quarter of a million miles. Obviously it had spiralled in closer during Earth's intervening history, by means either natural or artificial. I was interested to hear this idea of travel between worlds in space. I had once heard a vague story that at the time of the migrations to Killibol there was also communication with other worlds by means of giant missiles from Earth, but nobody on Killibol was much interested in space travel. For one thing, Killibol's sun had no other planets and so there was nowhere to go.

The people of Hesha waited in fear and trembling for the day when the Meramites would descend on them. The Meramites, they informed us, were a cruel and cold people without any sense of beauty. Becmath, on the contrary, was in high spirits when he heard of the invasion.

"There'll be confusion," he told me. "Maybe we can carve out a territory for ourselves."

But he made no move, although from everything we had seen we could have accounted well for ourselves in a fight. Earth weapons didn't seem to have the same weight as ours. The guns that had been used against us were long, slender tubes that fired darts. Once launched, the darts gained additional range from a tiny rocket charge. They could be lethal, but the weapon was a toy compared with our stuff.

I had to admit that Bec's analysis had been right: the inhabitants of Earth were of a softer, less sharp variety than those of Killibol. These people from Merame, however, were still an unknown quantity.

There were other nations, other intelligent species, maybe, elsewhere on Earth. But they were a long way off. Bec said we would stay here.

"We've found the load," he would say to me. "Now we've got to find the fulcrum."

In Klittmann the fulcrum meant two things: Protection (another word for direct intimidation) and the Squeeze (which meant you put your heel down on the only supply pipe of a much-needed commodity). Our taking over the village was the first kind, but we were too small to do that on a large scale. It had to be the second kind — or something new.

Naturally we didn't think it out that clearly at that time: our ideas were vague and unformed. The truth was that Bec was trying to get up the nerve to move out, to take the chance on hitting something bigger — teaming up with the invaders from the Moon, maybe. As it happened we did well to stay: because our fulcrum appeared from an unexpected, but logical, source.

I knew that Tone the Taker didn't have much pop left and I was waiting to see him finally go crazy, start screaming and kill himself with convulsions. Eventually he wasn't around for a while and I figured he must have crawled away to die. Not that I cared, and I was glad I didn't have to watch the spectacle, because I'd seen a pop addict get it before. It isn't pretty.

But suddenly Tone turned up again. "Hello, Tone," Bec said, surprised. "Where you been?"

"Living with the green people," Tone said, shrugging aimlessly. "Bec, I need a favour."

only part of his staff. I've told you, the Rotrox are trained to

"Oh, what's that?" We both looked at Tone curiously. By now he should have been dead. Instead, he looked better than he had any right to.

His face was tanned by the sunlight, of course. All our faces were. He was twitching, but not one half as much as he should have been. Correction: he shouldn't have been twitching at all. He should have been a corpse. Had the green people given him something, I wondered?

It seemed that they had. They used some kind of drug and Tone had found out about it with that famous nose of his. It eased his craving and kept the withdrawal symptoms at bay.

"Tell me about this stuff," Bec said, pointing Tone into a chair. "How do you take it?"

"It comes in a sort of a pad, like floss. It's soaked in it. You hold it over your nostrils and breathe in the fumes."

"You get some sort of charge out of it?"

"*They* do. It heightens their sensitivity. That's why they're so artistic. So gentle. It helps them see things a different way. But me —" he shrugged again — "it just takes away some of the pain."

"Sounds interesting. What do they call it?"

"In their language it means Blue Space. But it isn't blue, it's pink. They call it that because it gives them a feeling of endless blue space. that's what they say."

"Is it addictive, this stuff?" Bec's questions were pressing to an inexorable conclusion.

Tone nodded.

"And how many of the people here are addicted?"

"They all take it. Everybody in Rheatt."

"*Everybody?* In the whole country?"

Tone nodded again. "Everybody over eighteen years. You're not allowed it until then. It doesn't do much harm as long as you keep getting it."

Bec leaned back in his chair. "Well, I'll be damned."

Tone was getting restless. "You've got to help me, Bec—"

"Why?" Bec demanded harshly. "What the hell do you need? You've got your dope. What else do you need?"

"But it isn't strong enough!" Tone wrung his hands. "It helps, but not enough. I'm getting too used to it! Blue Space is watered down from some stronger stuff they don't let you use. I've got to have it!"

"They *refused* you this other stuff?" Bec asked wonderingly, concerned that the mob's authority didn't carry that far.

"They don't have it here. Their supply comes in once a year from some other place. It's already diluted. *You* tell them, Bec. *You* make them get it for me."

"Why should I?"

"For pity's sake! I *need* it. Remember how I helped you, Bec. I found Harmen for you."

"Sure, but what have you done for me lately?" Bec's lips were curled. He was enjoying making Tone squirm. "Why didn't you come and tell me about this dope before? You know dope is my business."

"I thought you knew . . . anyway it wouldn't do you any good. They get it free. They don't have to pay for it. It's like a public service."

"Where does it come from? Tell me where it comes from and I might do something for you."

I knew Bec was only exploring. He didn't care whether Tone got what he needed or not.

"It's all from one place. Some valley. That's the only place where the stuff will grow."

There was a moment's silence. "There's only one place where the stuff will grow," Bec repeated.

"All right, Tone," he said after another pause, "here's what you're going to do. You're going to find that valley where they grow Blue Space. Klein is going to come with you. That's the only way you're going to get the stuff you need, because nobody is going to bring it here for you. Understand?"

Tone was uncomfortable. "I don't know where it is."

"The green people here — do they know?"

"I think so. I'm not sure."

"Well, find out. The sooner you start the better. And not a word to your friends about what my interest is. Understand?"

Tone understood all right. He'd seen this kind of operation enough times before.

The best way to find where a source was was to get somebody who needed it bad. These people had a natural directional instinct. They were like bloodhounds and in their desperation could penetrate any screen. You did this by cutting off their usual supply and offering this one as their only hope. Tone had probably been put through the pipe before.

When Tone had shuffled out and left us alone in the drape-hung room Bec was laughing.

"Would you believe it!"

I stroked my chin. "It's certainly remarkable."

"You can say that again. It's all just the same here as it is on Killibol. I'll bet it's the same all over the damned universe. People falling into the same traps. Dope. Pop. Blue Space." He grunted. "The same old rackets will work every time."

"It is Earth, after all. Where we came from."

"Yeah, but a million years later."

"They're still human," I commented. "I guess humanity will always be the same, will always have the same weaknesses."

"I guess so. If this thing works out it could be big for us. How do you feel about the journey?"

"Nervous. Having to nurse the Taker and all. What do you want me to do?"

"Just scout this place and report back. Whether it's defended and whether you think we can take it. Try not to be conspicuous."

Looking at myself in a mirror, thinking of those thick black goggles I would be wearing (we had had better ones made in a native workshop), I wondered just how I was going to do that.

Seven

There was a road leading out of Hesha, winding over the horizon between low hills. We made the journey in a Rheattic carriage driven by a light motor that burned some kind of oil. Towed behind us was a trailer carrying enough of it to see us through.

We had a Heshan guide, too, who was supposed to know the way to the Blue Space Valley. He said it was five days' journey away. I asked him if he knew why we wanted to go there. He said no. I told him it was for the sake of my friend, who was very sick without the special drug he could get there. The guide looked very doleful and told me the concentrated drug could not be lawfully used.

While we travelled I wondered about a society completely swamped by a drug habit. Klittmann was riddled, of course, rotten with it, but only ever by a minority of people. Pop was a killer, raddling the body and distorting the mind. Blue Space, on the other hand, was comparatively mild in its effects. It seemed to induce a calm, fatalistic attitude in its users. The Rheattites had a fetish about beauty and beautiful things, and Blue Space seemed to open up their appreciation of them.

I thought to myself that maybe I would try it some time. A few doses couldn't hurt me. But I pushed the thought from my mind; how often had I heard people say the same about pop, only to turn up as pathetic wrecks a few years later? Besides, the attractiveness and harmlessness of the Rheattites wasn't going to stop Bec from putting the squeeze on them if he could. With my background and my associates it would be just as well not to become infected with their way of looking at things.

Only one incident in the outgoing journey is worth mentioning. We were crossing a flat, grassy plain. I heard a faint droning noise over our heads. Looking up, I saw something flying steadily across the sky from east to west.

At first I thought it was a bird, but its wings were stiff and it had a long metallic body. It could only be a machine. I got my repeater ready, but it made no attempt to attack us but merely flew on out of sight. Our guide told us not to worry; it was a Rheattic aircraft.

I wondered what else the green people had that we hadn't seen.

We left the road just before reaching the valley, which made our guide become suspicious and want to know why. I told him to shut up and lead the way.

The carriage wouldn't travel well over an unmade surface. We proceeded on foot and climbed up a steep slope, almost a mountain. It was covered in shale and nothing grew on it — something to do with the special qualities of the soil that allowed it alone to grow the Blue Space plants, I imagined. I thought of leaving our guide behind for the last stretch, but he might have lit out and caused us trouble. So I forced him down on his belly and we crawled the last few yards.

The slope ended abruptly and curved away on either side in a sharp ridge. Actually the valley wasn't a valley at all; it was a crater made by the impact of a meteor some thousands of years before. The slope on the other side was just as steep as the one we had scrambled up, but the depression was more shallow. There was a break in the crater wall, facing north, which I could see clearly and which the Rheattites used as an entrance.

The whole of the crater floor was made into an orchard of small trees with impossibly luxurious, petal-like blossoms, all pink and red. There were no trees remotely like them in Hesha. As soon as we poked our heads over the rim of the crater we got a face full of the perfume from these blossoms that almost lifted us into the air. It was a sickly sweet smell, rising straight up like a convection current.

Tone breathed it in and let out a shuddering, happy sigh. His system, straining with need, had recognised its panacea.

I spent some minutes inspecting the valley closely, specially the entrance. A fair-sized road came through it and branched out all over the crater. Some buildings lined the crater walls; probably places for processing the dope, I thought.

What I took to be barracks were lodged just inside the entrance, on either side of the road. They weren't very big, but I thought I'd better see what they had on the outside of the crater. Telling Tone and Heshan to stay put, I worked my way round. There were guards posted on the outside of the entrance, that was all. I was in time to see a couple of wagons leave the valley, turning to circle it by a road that left to the south.

According to what we had heard the valley was the producing and disseminating centre for a free public service, like protein was supposed to be (but wasn't) back on Killibol. There was no need, in Rheattic eyes, for it to be heavily guarded; to my more predatory mind it was ludicrously vulnerable, specially in time of war. If I had been the Rheattic commander I would have stationed an army there.

The place wasn't even very big. I judged the valley to be three miles in diameter. Bec was going to be pleased.

I slithered back to the others. "Let's be on our way," I said. "I think I've seen enough."

"Aren't we going in?" Tone asked pleadingly.

"Don't be stupid, Tone," I told him.

"But you know what I want. Bec promised—"

"You'll have to wait," I said bluntly. "We have to report to Bec first. You'll get your dope when we take the valley."

Tone stared down at the heady blossoms. His face looked like he was going to cry.

"Come on, move it!" I said harshly. "You've held out this long, you can hold out a bit longer." I turned to go.

We had been speaking Klittmann, but the Heshan had been watching our exchange closely. He stood up uncertainly on the loose shale.

"You come in secret and hide. You are not here for your friend. You mean some harm to Blue Space Valley."

"Pack it in, will ya?" I glared from one to the other, surreptitiously loosening the strap that held my repeater on my back.

The Heshan backed away. "Let us go openly through the gate. I do not have to hide. I will go and tell them you are here."

I had to give him a score for guts. He set off down the outer slope at a slithering run. I yelled for him to stop, and reached for my repeater.

But Tone had grabbed my elbow. "I'm sorry, Klein, I can't go away now. Not when it's so close. Just lemme—"

He broke off and scrambled over the lip of the crater. I made a grab for him but it was too late.

Cursing, I turned back to the Heshan, who was making good time down the slope now. If he made it to the entrance I would be in trouble. I took careful aim. My repeater hammered loudly. The Heshan took a tumble, the slugs knocking him yards further down the slope, and lay still.

I flung myself to the crater brim, thinking I might still be in time to stop Tone. For a moment or two the sun flashed straight into my eye-shades, dazzling me. Then I saw him. He wasn't running or clambering but rolling down the inside slope, plunging helter-skelter towards those blossoms that he hoped would give him peace of mind.

Already he was a long way off. I threw a long burst from the repeater after him. The sound echoed across the valley. Then Tone was lost to sight beneath the pink and red blooms and I wasn't sure if I had hit him.

I quickly discarded the idea of going after him. A lot of people down in the crater might already have heard my repeater going off. There were too many of them. The only thing I could do now was get back to Hesha.

Making the journey back alone was kind of lonely, a little frightening. I'd never been left alone in the middle of an Earth landscape before, seven days from my own people. But I made it without any trouble and gave Bec the news.

"So you think this valley is wide open?" he asked after I'd finished.

"Looks like it. Of course, they might have some way of sealing off the entrance that I didn't see — a metal door or a rock fall. But I reckon we could be through before they have time to use it. The sloop could get over the wall of the crater in any case."

"Hmm. Do you think Tone will talk if he's still alive?"

"It's hard to say. Not willingly, because he knows we're going to turn up sooner or later and he doesn't want us to have a score to settle. But if they hold the stuff out on him he'll do anything."

Bec nodded. "It's a chance we'll have to take. We have to move fast anyway. Things are happening."

"Oh?" I had noticed that things didn't seem quite the same in the village. The atmosphere was more subdued, more quiet.

"Somebody came to the village to say that the Meramites are moving this way. The locals are pretty scared. They're asking us to fight the Meramites for them." He chuckled.

"So how do we handle it?" I asked.

"The first thing is to move on Blue Space Valley to give us some property to bargain with. I guess I should really send you to do that job, but I want you to stay here with me. Give Grale and the others the low-down and they can sort it out."

"It's liable to get pretty hot around here, boss. After all we don't know an awful lot about what these Moon guys can do."

"We'll play it by ear," he said, unperturbed.

The sloop left the next day. I didn't feel nearly so self-confident without it. Bec had given Harmen the option of leaving with the sloop or staying. He elected to stay and Bec conceived a plan for him to help us make contact.

"We might need an amount of bluff here," he explained. "It won't do for them to meet the boss straight away. We'll use Harmen for a front man. You know the old 'Organisation Routine'? You think you've met the top man, then suddenly you find out he's not the top man and you find yourself faced with somebody he's dirt to. It makes a good impression."

He grinned sourly. "Besides, it might save us from getting our heads blown off."

We prepared a bunker at the opposite end of the village to that which the Meramites were approaching. Bec posted lookouts. He told the villagers he would handle things for them, but that was only to secure their co-operation. I guess they were better off with Bec in charge, though. He told them not to resist but to surrender, sending out envoys to say that the village was in the hands of an alien power not of Rheatt.

He had reckoned without the Meramites' way of doing things, however. Hesha was only a small village to them, an outpost of a nation they had already conquered, and they believed in a policy of punishment-in-advance. From the hillside we watched the approach of the Meramite column, sending up a cloud of dust. The Meramites were riding on wheeled platforms, circular in shape, carrying about twenty men apiece. They stopped not far outside the village and we saw our messengers deliver their news. We saw them slaughter those messengers and then roll forward mercilessly.

"Get to the bunker," Bec said in clipped tones. "This isn't going to be so easy."

A withering fire swept the village, starting fires here and there. The Meramite soldiery carried lance-like poles that fired gouts of hot metal. You could just about see them when they shot from the tip of the lance, streaking out like a line of light. They didn't seem to be very accurate, but they didn't have to be in the circumstances.

We made it to the bunker through clouds of smoke. It was a well-set-up position at the end of the main street, backed up by solid brick buildings. Its upper parts, jutting up above the road, had a step-like construction, one block being set more forward than the other, and into these two blocks we had set the Jains. The arrangement gave absolute command of the street ahead of us and good control over the environs, each gun being able to cover the other from attack from any side.

Bec thrust guns into the hands of Harmen and two Heshans we had trained to use repeaters. We nestled down behind the Jains, peering through the firing slits in their shields.

"Here they come!" yelled Bec. "Let 'em have it!"

The Meramite carrier platforms appeared at the other end of the wide street. We saw big grey figures, considerably bigger than the Rheattites, arrogantly directing their glowing lances this way and that, indulging in the arbitrary destruction we later came to expect of them.

We let them get well into the street before letting loose. They scarcely knew what had hit them. Deadly though their hot-lead poles were, they just weren't in the same class as a pair of good Jains, the most effective, withering machine-guns ever designed. An almost solid sheet of lead ripped down the length of the street, the racket reverberating between the walls of the houses with a noise like ten thousand rivet-guns. We put in a mixture of explosive and spin-bullets, too. You can do a variety of such mixtures on a Jain gun, say one explosive, one spin to every ten straight. If a spin-bullet hits you it more or less turns you into a jelly.

Our blast lasted only seconds. We had to watch the ammo. But the Meramites were wiped out, their riding platforms leaning crazily.

"That'll show them they're up against something," Bec grinned.

Three times they tried to send men down the street, with the same result. We were beginning to conclude that the Meramites weren't too bright, or else weren't very skilled in war. By now the village was blazing merrily. We could hear screams and the *zip-zip* of the hot-lead poles. I wondered if they treated every village this way or if it was only us they were after.

A few times they tried to infiltrate in from the sides but couldn't get at us until our ammunition ran out, and we had enough to last for a while. However, this wasn't quite as Bec had planned it, as far as I knew. We were bound to run out eventually.

I looked across at him. "Still planning on contact?"

"Sure."

"Mind telling me how?"

Bec's goggles scanned the street. "Leave it for a while. They'll start thinking things out themselves pretty soon."

This time he was right. There was another movement at the far end of the street. A tall, broad Meramite was waving a banner.

We held our fire as he strode nearer with an odd, jerky gait. He held the banner aloft on a tall pole. It depicted a man hanging upside down, suspended by his feet.

"It is a flag of truce," one of the Heshans told us. "They want to talk."

"Good," said Bec. He climbed down from his Jain and relieved the Heshan of his repeater. "Get out there and tell him a representative of the Great Powers of Klittmann will speak to one of equal rank, if such an officer will present himself."

"Hey, Bec," I said, speaking Klittmann. "You know what they did to the last Heshans we sent out."

"Sure, but it's different now. Out you go, man."

He gave the Heshan a hefty shove to help him on his way. The poor guy was so scared he was shaking, but he climbed out and bravely walked towards the Meramite with the banner.

The two of them looked strange together. Rheattites tended to be slightly taller than we are, but the invaders from the Moon were taller still. They averaged seven to eight foot. But they looked kind of lank and weak, thyroidal. They made me wonder how they managed to stand up. Later I found it wasn't so easy for them.

Their skins were slate-grey and so were their uniforms. Their broad chests were criss-crossed with black straps that made them look sinister and powerful. The truce-maker didn't kill our Heshan, as I had half-expected, but listened while the green-skinned man, staring up at him like a child, delivered our message. Nodding curtly, he turned and walked away.

Minutes later the banner-bearer returned with a companion who strode haughtily before him, walking unconcernedly over the bodies of his dead soldiers. Unlike the banner-bearer, he wore a helmet with designs on it. I couldn't make out from this distance. Stopping some yards in front of our foremost Jain, he stood with legs astride, thumbs hooked in a waist-belt.

Meanwhile the Heshan had thankfully returned to the bunker. "Your turn now, Harmen," Bec said, a hint of amusement in his voice. "Get out there and make yourself look like somebody big. Tell him we represent the powers of Klittmann, another world. Say we have no quarrel with the men of Merame and for that reason have not opposed their conquest of Rheatt. Say we expect the same respect from them. Then tell him that if he is merely a subordinate officer he must stay outside and talk to you, but if he is of exalted rank and a leader of his people he may come inside the bunker and speak to me. Make it clear that I won't make agreements with an underling."

The alchemist looked at him for long, brooding moments, his long hair hanging lankly down his shoulders. If nothing else, I thought, he would make a strong impression on the Meramites by his appearance alone.

But he had been brought a long way against his will. He had been involved in a lot of things he didn't want to be involved in, and now Bec was making him carry out negotiations for him. He didn't like it much.

"Am I your messenger boy?" he said. "Your mummer?"

"You're not in a position to make choices," Bec stated. "Get up there and do what I say." He paused. "Maybe you *are* in a position to make choices, at that. See if you can make your own private deal with the Meramites. Maybe they'll give you a big laboratory. But remember, Harmen: I've promised you a big laboratory, too. A real big one. You know what the game is, so serve my purpose."

Bec said all this in a flat, disinterested tone. He was obviously referring to private conversations the two had held. Reluctantly the alk heaved himself up out of the bunker.

I watched him talking to the Meramite. The other was clearly taken aback by his appearance. The eye-shades probably convinced him that we were, indeed, something new and alien. Eventually Harmen pointed back to the bunker, addressing a question in a loud, gruff voice. The Meramite raised his voice, also, and a disdainful smile passed fleetingly across his lips. After a short altercation he followed Harmen towards the bunker.

Bec signalled me to stay up with the nearside Jain, which put me sitting up over his head from where he sat in a padded chair in the recesses of the bunker. The Meramite bent his head and almost doubled up to enter. I heard funny little *chinking* sounds as he came on by me, then I couldn't see him any more. I continued to keep a look-out, listening to the conversation going on behind me.

The Meramite spoke Rheattic, but in a clipped, supercilious accent and in a voice that was incongruously high-pitched for someone of his size. All the Meramites, I found later, had that high-pitched, child's voice.

"I am Commander of the Rheattic Border Expeditionary Force," he said. "I am here to speak with your leader."

There was a scraping noise as the Heshans drew up a bench for him to sit on. "My name is Becmath," Bec drawled. "Sit down."

The other did so. "You claim to represent a foreign power. Not on Earth?"

"No."

"Or Merame?"

"No."

"Mars, then? Venus? I have never heard of any journeying from those worlds."

"We're not from there either. We're not from any world you can see in the sky. But enough of that. My quarrel with you is that you have destroyed this village, which I had taken for my own."

"When your messenger first came to us," the other replied, "we had taken his claim to be a lie, a desperate subterfuge, and so we meted out heavier punishment than we might otherwise have done. We have reasons not to make our destruction of the country too complete, but we must subjugate. Now that we have seen the effects of your weapons, however, as well as your un-Rheattic appearance. . . . It is very dark in here, yet you cover your eyes. Light hurts you, perhaps?"

"How would you like to have such weapons?" Bec said, ignoring the last question.

"Oh, we will. We will."

The Meramite's answer came as a surprise. I heard a choking gasp. Turning round, I saw the visitor sitting across from me, his knees drawn up, his thin lips bunched up in a smile that seemed to distort his flat, gigantic face. It was a smile of complacent triumph. Bec, Harmen and the two Heshans were folding up and falling to the floor.

At the same time something sharp thrilled in my nostrils and throat. My nerves tingled. I tried to move, but couldn't. The Meramite had released some sort of gas into the bunker, a gas which left him unaffected.

My last thought as I passed out was that we had been outmanoeuvred. The Meramites knew some angles, too. We had been taken.

Eight

High-pitched voices. Mingled background noises. Chinking sounds coming from all round.

I opened my eyes to find myself trussed up and lying on the ground. Painfully I forced myself to a sitting position. Becmath and Harmen were already awake nearby, sitting upright with their hands tied behind their backs. Harmen, as so often, had withdrawn into himself, his head bowed. Bec grimaced as he saw I was conscious.

"I guess Hesha was harder to hang on to than it was to take," he said.

My head cleared quickly. We were in one of the big meadows outside Hesha. Meramite troop carriers were parked all round us. The grey, lank soldiery went about their business with a peculiar loping gait, tending machines I hadn't seen before, or merely stood around.

It seemed that the chinky sounds happened every time they walked. For the first time I noticed that they wore on their arms and legs a kind of open harness made of metal rods. As they moved the rods worked in a piston-like action. This puzzled me, but I didn't stop to think about it at the time.

Smoke from the burning village blew over the scene. I coughed, then looked up to see the Meramite officer who had slipped us the knock-out gas standing over us.

I stared into his flat, grey face: thin lips, large, heavy jaw, wide vacant cheeks, oddly flat grey eyes that were without any trace of humour or expression, as if no mind lay behind them.

Suddenly the alk raised his head. "So this is what you understand by a flag of truce," he said accusingly.

The Meramite's lips curved in the faintest sneer. "Subterfuge is a weapon. We did not have to use it. We could have summoned heavier equipment to blast you out. But we wished to capture your weaponry undamaged."

He paused, then continued: "We have searched the village for others of your kind, but found none. Despite that, the villagers have not been slow to talk. They say you have other forces which left a few days ago. Where did they go?"

"You'll be hearing from them," Bec said. His voice sounded faraway and unreal.

For the first time I began to feel a loss of confidence in Bec. He looked like an insignificant, squat figure alongside the looming Meramite. The other listened to his answer, stared as if he didn't understand, then glanced over his shoulder. Following his glance, I saw something approaching from the distance, sailing low above the ground. It was a big cylinder, part silver and part copper in colour, bevelled at either end and finished off in flattened points.

"You will be taken to our main camp on the central plain of Rheatt," our captor told us. "There your answers will be made more meaningful — you may even meet the persons of exalted rank you desire. I pity you. Merame has only one use for prisoners."

The cylinder settled on the grass. "Here comes your transport. Now we shall see how you can be of service to the Rotrox."

Cold, clammy hands lifted us and carried us into the cylinder. We sat on a metal deck, leaning against the curved walls, guarded by the gigantic soldiers. I felt the machine lift into the air with a slight droning sound.

"What do we do now?" I said hoarsely to Bec.

He shifted uneasily. "It all depends on whether the boys got to Blue Space Valley in time. If the Meramites got there first. . . ." He shrugged.

We seemed to fly for quite a while. About halfway through the journey our guards opened a hatch in the floor and gazed through it with interest, smiling. One glanced at me, speaking to his companions in a strange language. What he said seemed to please them. He came across and dragged me nearer the hatch, so that I, too, could see through it.

We were passing leisurely over a level plain. Through it wound a seemingly endless column of wretched Rheattites strung together by chains. Many of them appeared to be dead or unconscious but were still dragged along helplessly by their fellows. The column was policed by Meramites riding smaller versions of the circular transport platforms. Shouts, screams and the sharp crack of whips floated up to us. I saw upturned green faces watching our passage. On either side of me the guards uttered cruel, humourless chuckles.

Then they thought of a new sport. One grabbed me by the legs and another under the armpits, and I was swung out over the open hatch. The breeze tugged at me. They jigged me up and down, pretending to let go. I closed my eyes. I didn't think a couple of rank and file klugs would have the nerve to murder a prisoner in their charge, but I didn't know much about how Meramites behave. I was scared.

I felt a lurch, for a split second felt myself sailing through the air, then fell roughly to the deck again. The guards sniggered.

"Take it easy, Klein," Bec murmured. "We'll have our turn."

The people of Rheatt didn't build cities. Their civilisation was more dispersed, more rural. They did have centres of loose concentration, however — what would pass for cities for them. We flew over the main one and were able to see something of it through the open hatch.

It was like a vast park stretching beyond the horizon in all directions. There were broad walks, gardens and groves. The buildings were few and scattered, and consisted mostly of tall, delicate green towers.

The scene would have been a really pretty one had it not been for the fact that the Meramites had chosen to set up their main camp there. A maze of continuous, low corridor-like buildings sprawled across the park and snaked between the green towers, rather like a system of tunnels built above the ground. Their colour was grey, the same as everything else about the Meramites.

I was beginning to realise that we from Killibol had more in common with the Meramites than with the people of Rheatt. Like us, they had a distaste for the open. They were city dwellers, ruthless, smart and practical. If anything, they were several degrees more vicious. I hoped this meant that they had a streak of stupidity in their make-up, the kind that Bec would know how to take advantage of.

The flying cylinder slanted down and came to rest. We were manhandled on to one of the circular vehicles and wheeled into the corridor complex. These corridors reminded me of endless barracks. They were lit by a strange whitish illumination, quite unlike the light outside. Uniformed Meramites stared at us in puzzlement as we were carried along.

The angles at which some of the corridors branched off at the intersections told me that the invaders had also been busy digging underground. They also, maybe, hid away from the sun.

We were thrown into a darkened room and lay there for a short while. I asked Bec if he had any ideas. He said just to keep cool, to take my cue from him, and if left on my own not to say anything even if they got rough. I asked Harmen if *he* had any ideas. The alk just grunted.

The door opened and they dragged away Bec. Shortly afterwards the door opened again.

"Which one is Klein?" the tall figure in the doorway said in his boyish voice.

"I am," I said, and immediately was jerked to my feet and the ropes binding them cut. "I'll be seeing you," I said to Harmen, "I hope."

They led me down a sloping passage and into a large, fairly luxurious room. Bec was there, without his eye-shades and with his eyes tightly closed against the glare. His jacket and shirt had been ripped off. Blood ran down his side from where a torturer's instruments had been at work. The torturer stood on one side of the room, the bloody pincers still in his hands.

But he was only a bit player in the scene. Bec faced an even larger than average Meramite who sat behind a table on which were laid devices that were strange to me. I guessed immediately that he was a big shot. Behind him stood two more companions, themselves of high rank judging by their insignia, but who stood respectfully at attention.

Bec's face was drawn, but he had evidently managed to control the pain. His blind face turned towards me.

"Is that you, Klein?" he asked, speaking Klittmann.

"That's right, Bec," I answered.

"I want you to meet Chief Imnitrin, grand commander of the invasion forces and one of the big chiefs up on Merame. I insisted on having you here so you would know what was going on." To the Meramite, in Rheattite, he said: "Now we can talk. But first the covers for my eyes."

Chief Imnitrin nodded. The torturer stepped forward and placed the goggles in Bec's hands. He fumbled them over his eyes and looked around himself slowly. The torturer, meanwhile, was applying some kind of tape-like stuff to the wounds he had caused. The bleeding stopped.

Imnitrin looked at me. "Your leader withstands pain and does not answer our questions. We Rotrox respect men who withstand pain. Of course, it has not yet been proved of you."

"It's just their way of breaking the ice, Klein," Bec told me grimly. "Just a shaking of hands, as it were. I don't think they'll start on you."

For a moment my mind went back to Klittmann. I remembered a small room back of the garages where we wound a wire round some guy and jolted the electricity in. It was just a way of getting information. Mob men like us were not strangers to torture.

As I contrasted that scene with the one before my eyes I realised that there was a difference. In Klittmann we were purely direct and masculine: it was all technique. There was something frighteningly eerie, almost effeminate, about these big ungainly Meramites. I formed the impression that they probably had all kinds of fetishes and incomprehensible pleasures.

"You are here to speak with me," Imnitrin rebuked sharply, "not to converse with one another. You mentioned advantages in our meeting. Speak forth. Tell me from where you come."

"I am also full of curiosity about *you*," Bec replied brashly. "I presume you have reasons for invading Rheatt. Let us talk of those."

Imnitrin shrugged, as if it was a foolish question whose answer was already known. "Is it not obvious? The Rotrox tribe, having conquered all nations and sectors of Merame, determines to extend its empire to Earth. We shall gain slaves, much wealth, natural resources not found on Merame. Soon many nations of Earth will feel the boot of Rotrox."

"And you thought Rheatt would make an ideal bridgehead, didn't you? A soft people, easily subdued. But it hasn't gone quite according to plan, has it?"

The other frowned slightly. "The Rheattites are not well practised in war, it is true . . . but you are mistaken to call them soft. Have you found them so? Perhaps with your weapons. . . . But in a border village you will not have encountered the fighting men of Rheatt, the airmen and the infantry. These we enjoyed the sport of crushing. Furthermore the battle is not yet won. Extra forces mass beyond Rheatt's borders. A great fight is ahead. Nothing, however, can withstand the might of Rotrox."

"Sure, you win all the battles," Bec said, chuckling in spite of his pain, "but what about afterwards? An empire's no good if you can't make any use of it, is it?"

The Meramite stood up and chinked round the table, looming over Bec. "You speak insolently, yet with knowledge." For a moment he leaned threateningly over Bec, as if he would reach out and squash him with one huge hand. Then he stood back pensively.

"It is as you say. Some disease seems to afflict the Rheattites once they are conquered. Their spirits are broken. They cannot be made to work. They merely lie around and die, no matter how much we beat them."

"And you really don't know why? Bec asked, seemingly amused.

Imnitrin shrugged. "Their spirits are broken."

Bec uttered a short, sharp laugh. "I thought so!" Turning to me, he said in Klittmann: "These people are pretty hamfisted, Klein. They don't do their research properly — they don't even know about Blue Space."

Turning back to Imnitrin, he went on: "I can make the Rheattites into useful slaves for you. I can help you win that last battle. As it's their last effort the Rheattites will put their all into it. Who knows, you might even lose — without our help."

"How will you do this?" the other demanded suspiciously. "With new weapons? New torments for the Rheattite slaves?"

"Nothing so crude. The Rheattites are dependent on a drug they take. If they can't get it they fall to pieces. When you conquer a region the people inside have their supply cut off. You've seen what happens."

Imnitrin looked sharply at his officers, then back at Bec. "You speak truly? Or shall I call for more torturers? ..."

"I'm telling you the truth," Bec said firmly. His voice rose. "How is it you don't already know this? Did you not enquire why the Rheattites seemed to become ill?"

"Our task is conquest, not to enquire after the health of slaves," Imnitrin sneered mincingly. "If there is truth in your explanation, we shall appoint Rheattite slave-administrators to deal with it. Men of the Rotrox Tribe do not soil their hands with such matters. Indeed, once our Earth Empire is founded there are few who would wish to spend their time here." He retreated back behind the table and seated himself, his expression becoming dour and gloomy. With the odd, slightly inhuman cast of the Meramite face it made him look almost tearful. "Here the air is too thick, all objects are too heavy, and outlines are blurred and difficult to see. Perhaps you, who claim also to hail from another world, appreciate how unpleasant Earth is."

Bec nodded. "I'm glad we are agreed on one thing. Perhaps we can agree on other things. I can supply the drug the Rheattites need to your slaves and subject populations, making the supply dependent on their co-operation and good behaviour. An addict will do anything to get . . . well, maybe you're not familiar with that aspect of human affairs. I can also cut off the supply from the forces that oppose you, reducing their fighting efficiency almost to zero. This drug, though you haven't realised it yet, is the means to the most perfect control over the whole of Rheatt."

He paused, giving the Meramite commander time to think. Then, forcefully and loudly, he said: "It is we, not you, who have that control."

"For such impertinence you should die," the other said coldly. "What the men of Rotrox want, they take. You say you control the drug? We will take it from you. If necessary we will manufacture it ourselves, using Rheattite technicians."

"I'm afraid not." Slowly and carefully Bec explained about Blue Space Valley, the one and only source of Rheattite dope. He finished by bringing me into the conversation. "Klein, tell them what orders our boys in the valley have."

"To destroy everything and burn the orchards if anybody tries to get in. It's quite easy to do: the valley isn't very large. Either me or Bec has to turn up or there won't be any Blue Space any more."

"You should know that my men are very efficient and always carry out their orders," Bec put in.

Imnitrin glanced round at his officers as if inviting comment. One of them stirred.

"Your story is ridiculous. We will simply set up production of the trees elsewhere."

"They won't grow anywhere else," I explained. "The valley was created by a meteor impact. The meteor must have contained special minerals that enable the trees to synthesise the drug, because they're a peculiar strain that's evolved there alone. They won't grow anywhere else. I guess if you did take over the valley eventually from our men you might find some seeds that had survived and could grow a new crop then, but that would take years."

Big meteors occasionally fell on Killibol. Everybody knew of the one that had destroyed the city of Chingak, spreading radio-active wastes for miles around.

"You can check these facts with the Rheattites themselves — as you should have done long ago," Bec supplemented. "Well, that's the position, Commander. Now let's talk terms."

"Your behaviour is threatening and insolent."

"I don't see it that way," Bec said, smiling. "We're here to help you, not to harm you. Our interests are identical. Why, already we've made you better off than you were before. You know about the Blue Space drug and why your slaves aren't able to work. You can even find out where the valley is."

"Very well. What *are* your interests?" Imnitrin leaned over the table. I saw that despite his indulgence in answering Bec's questions, despite the blunders and oversights that were typical of his race, he was hard, calculating and merciless. "You have not yet answered *our* questions. Where is your planet? Do you also plan invasion of Earth? What do you want here?"

"Our planet is so far away that it can't be seen in the sky," Bec answered. "It's in another galaxy, if you know what galaxies are. There's a special way of getting to it which only we know. As for your other questions, I may as well be perfectly frank. Then you'll know you can trust me. We're not here to conquer Earth; quite the reverse. No more of my people will be coming from our own planet. There are only us you have prisoner and my other men, with more powerful weapons you haven't seen, in Blue Space Valley. We are outcasts from our own world. Our wish is to make a place for ourselves here and eventually to raise strong forces to return to our own planet and destroy our enemies. So that's what we can offer you, Commander: not only the means to rule Rheatt with ease but also a new world to conquer, with our help. In return we wish to be given positions of honour in your empire."

It looked as if Imnitrin was going to spit. "Men of other tribes are not honoured by the Rotrox. It would be necessary to swear oaths of allegiance."

"That's fine by me, Commander Imnitrin. We'll swear allegiance. We'll become men of the tribe of Rotrox."

Imnitrin gazed at us thoughtfully, speculatively.

Nine

A few weeks later I stood with Becmath, Imnitrin and three of his high-ranking officers, looking at the battleground below through the open side of one of their flying cylinders.

The plain was flanked by gently rising hills to our left, and broke into a series of gullies on the right. All morning Rheatite infantry had been filing into the plain, advancing towards the Rotrox columns camped at one end.

Imnitrin peered down at the massing Rheattites. "They are many, and well-armed," he said in his chilling, incisive voice. "Could it be that your plan has gone wrong?"

"We'll find that out when the fighting starts," Bec answered gruffly.

We were floating about fifty feet above a round-topped hill. A few other cylinders drifted slowly above the landscape, casting shadows on the green-skinned Rheattites. Behind us in the cavernous interior of the cylinder was Rotrox communications equipment: oval screens of a pale blue colour, like icy mirrors, surmounting grey metal cabinets.

The television system had quite startled me when I first saw it in operation. We had vision phones back in Klittmann, but their definition was crude and blurred compared with the Rotrox sets. The Rotrox could send in colour, too, but the colours came out odd and wrong. Most surprising, they used Hertzian transmission without wires. On Killibol wireless sending of sound or pictures was never considered a practicable proposition, but then we lacked Earth's ionosphere. The Rotrox, however, used television even to keep in touch with their Council of Chiefs back on Merame.

It was funny, I thought, how the Rotrox were ahead of us

in some things but so backward in others. I guess different life styles produce different technologies.

I picked up a telescope to scan the faces of the Rheattites. They didn't seem to be as shaky as we had hoped. I knew Bec was worried. A lot hung on the outcome of this battle.

My mind went back over the past few weeks. Bec's gamble had paid off. The Rotrox had allowed him to send me to Blue Space Valley with a television transceiver and I had arrived to find Grale, Reeth and Hassmann firmly in command. Tone the Taker was there, too — my bullets had missed him — but he was barely conscious. The stuff he was taking now had put him in a permanent trance. The expression on his face was something dreamy and weird.

Straight away Bec had shown his genius for administration. He drew up a plan for distributing Blue Space to the populations under Rotrox control, sending me detailed instructions on what to give each collector that called. Using both Rheattites and Meramites, he was already setting up a pusher organisation, holding the Rheattite population in a rigid web of supply and demand. At one stroke he had begun the process of drawing the strings of power towards his own person.

The Rotrox were impressed. They admired success, by whatever method. Bec had a knack of getting along with them and they co-operated with his suggestions. Consequently we had all (leaving aside Tone and Harmen) taken oaths of fealty, mingling our blood with that of Imnitrin himself. The ceremony was pretty messy and the wound in my arm still hadn't healed. But we belonged to the Rotrox Tribe now.

Imnitrin had made an attempt to put Blue Space Valley in Rotrox hands. Bec had firmly resisted the idea and in the end the Meramites, realising that we had to be cautious on our own account, had not pressed the matter. Reeth and Hassmann were still there now, making sure nothing sneaky happened behind our backs.

Bec had instantly cut off the pipeline to the army massing further along the border. Why they hadn't taken the trouble to invest and hold Blue Space Valley themselves is just another example of Rheattite ineptness — but it had become clear that they already had reserves of the dope. Not enough to be completely happy, perhaps, but enough not to be falling over themselves the way we had hoped. Bec had practically promised the invaders victory and if they didn't get it their attitude towards us would change. They might even wipe us out. If they won, on the other hand, they would treat us like brothers. To try to lower the opposition's morale Bec had sent in agents to pass the word around that there would be Blue Space available if the Rheattites threw down their arms, surrendered or even simply lost.

Imnitrin was also using a telescope, studying, not the ground, but the sky. "The enemy approaches," he announced. "Battle begins."

He stepped further back into the cylinder and began speaking into the television apparatus in the clipped Rotrox tongue. Sweeping over the horizon, fairly high in the sky, was a squadron of Rheattite fighter aircraft. They were similar to the machine I had seen earlier but appeared somewhat smaller and moved more swiftly. At the same time a great shout went up from the horde below and the infantry began to advance.

The half dozen or so flying cylinders that all the time had been drifting harmlessly over the army took this as their cue and began dropping explosives and gas bombs. The gases — not used extensively for fear they would reach our own side — were almost instantly dispersed by the stiff breeze that crossed the plain and did little harm. The explosives flared in red, smoky blasts and took care of a score of men at a time.

I was mildly surprised at the unambitious nature of this bombardment. Why had the Rotrox not sprung hundreds of flying cylinders on the Rheattites, loaded to the roof with bombs, and annihilated them from the air? But when I looked at the type of ground weapons both sides had, I realised they were suffering from a rigidity of thinking. In the minds of both the Meramites and the Rheattites, warfare meant primarily close combat. Neither the fire-lances of the Rotrox nor the dart-guns of the Rheattites were accurate at long range, and neither did they pack much of a punch. The combatants stalked one another at close quarters or else fired away at one another at close range, coming swiftly in to grapple with knives if neither was successful. This style of fighting took little account of the type of efficient killing machine we had brought with us from Killibol.

With startling rapidity the fighter aircraft were among us. They were able to twist and turn in the air with considerable agility. Mounted on the front of their fuselages, just below the cockpit, they carried launching tubes which fired explosive rockets.

The Rotrox evidently had respect for these skilled aerial fighters. They themselves had atmospheric fighters of a clumsier kind, a great number of which had been launched in mid-air as the invasion fleet came in. Because of their superior numbers they had succeeded in virtually wiping out the Rheattite air force, but at great cost. What we saw now were the defenders' last few craft, and the Rotrox had decided not to pit their own surviving flying machines against them.

Instead, Bec had volunteered our services. He gave me a signal. I climbed up a short ladder. At the same time the side of the cylinder closed up like an eyelid, leaving only a narrow horizontal slot running the length of the vessel.

I emerged on to a small platform mounted atop the cylinder. One of our Hacker cannon from the sloop had been fitted there, complete with a personnel shield and a full magazine.

I scrambled behind the cannon and took a good look round me. The fighters were attacking the cylinders, downing them like ninepins. None of the other cylinders seemed to have any means of defending themselves. I saw one tip over and crash to the ground, breaking up under the impact of exploding rockets.

Then I swung the Hacker round fast. A fighter craft was howling towards me, lining up its rocket tube. I'm pretty good with a Hacker. I put my eye to the sight and pressed the button. A hard stream of shells hammered out. The fighter disintegrated in a cloud of flame, raining fragments all around.

I grinned tightly, traversing the Hacker and scanning the sky. The platform underneath me was rock steady, had hardly wavered in the blast. I began to feel good.

Most of the other cylinders were going down now. I adjusted the sight and trained on an aircraft just coming out of an attack dive about a mile and a half away. Only one or two of the shells found their targets but one of its wings dropped off and the machine tumbled earthwards, spinning end over end.

These fighter craft were nimble but they were flimsy. Just one well-placed Hacker shell was enough to send them flying to pieces. I downed another at fairly long range before they realised where the danger lay. Then two aircraft turned their noses towards me and came up fast. A rocket whanged over my head and exploded some distance behind me. The fighter it had come from followed moments later, on fire and already disintegrating from the hammering I had given it. Flaming fuel splashed down on to the cylinder. For a few seconds I was confused and could see nothing. Then I glimpsed the second fighter howling towards me and hastily tried to train the barrel of the Hacker on it.

But before I pressed the firing button the aircraft exploded into fragments.

I took a look at the ground. The shots had come from another Hacker, wielded by a Rotrox gunner in the sloop, which was emerging from one of culverts on the right of the battleground. I was surprised to know I probably owed my life to one of those grey monsters.

There was only one fighter aircraft left and it was hightailing it for the horizon. I decided to get back inside; the bulk of the cylinder was obscuring my view of the ground and I wanted to get a good look at the action.

Now that the air attack was over the longitudinal slot was gaping open again. I nodded to Bec as I came down, then peered over the rim of the slot.

The sloop had entered the fight at the right moment. The Rheattite infantry had pressed against the Meramite columns, which presented a disciplined diagonal array, and the battleline had swiftly degenerated into a bloody scrum, contained on one side by the line of hills. Into the Rheattite reserves, from their exposed side and from the rear, plunged the sloop.

Grale was driving. The guns were manned by Rotrox we had previously trained, taking out some of the fittings so that they were able to squat on the floor and fit their ungainly bulk into the interior.

I estimated that the combatants numbered roughly ten thousand on each side. The effect of the sloop's armoury on the massed Rheattites was devastating. The Jains and Hackers, as well as smaller portable repeaters fired through the gun-slits, cut them down in hundreds. Grale drove recklessly, churning over piles of bodies to penetrate more deeply into the mass.

The Rheattites had nothing to fight back with, either. They piled up on one another, pushing in a mob to get away from the death-dealing machine. Further in the rear some of the more enterprising began to bring up heavier weapons using explosives; but we had already checked that out and knew they would have little effect: the explosives used on both Earth and Merame were of a crude, low-impact type. The sloop's armour could take it.

Consternation and then panic began to spread through the Rheattite ranks. The appearance of this unfamiliar and apparently invincible weapon made a crack in their already shaky morale. Urged on by their officers, the Rotrox took the initiative and pressed the offensive, their fire-lances spitting cascades of hot metal into the green-skinned ranks. Steadily, inexorably, the long disciplined lines of extended lances advanced across the plain.

By now the Rheattites were beginning to mill up the slopes of the hills. For a moment it looked as though they would break; but somehow, miraculously, they held and began to reform, despite the continuing carnage wreaked by the sloop. The gunners had orders to keep killing until the ammunition was exhausted — which meant that, except for a few magazines cautiously kept safe in Blue Space Valley, we would be out of it altogether.

Then a new band of Rotrox appeared on a hilltop. These were not warriors, but technicians. With practised skill they erected a series of huge loudspeakers facing the battle-locked armies. A vast voice boomed out — a Rheattite voice, using a minion Bec had found:

"MEN OF RHEATT! THE DAY IS LOST — LAY DOWN YOUR ARMS! BLUE SPACE WILL BE ISSUED TO ALL WHO SURRENDER AND YOU WILL BE ALLOWED TO GO PEACEFULLY TO YOUR HOMES!"

The message was repeated again and again. At first it was ignored; then a few listened. Soon the temptation was spreading like fire. As Bec had gambled, thousands of the Rheattites were in fact badly in need of the drug. They had been prepared to fight in the hope of victory, but now that such hope seemed to be fading their will to resist was weak. Men came staggering up the hill, throwing away their weapons. Turning, I saw Imnitrin smiling his sinister smile.

"The rot begins!" he chimed. "I think the day is ours, brother Becmath."

Bec and I glanced at one another. Despite our affiliation into the tribe, Imnitrin had refrained until now from using the term "brother". Now, we knew, we were really in.

Down below the sloop fell silent, its magazines empty.

They took three thousand prisoners, thousands more fleeing.

The Rotrox herded them into a vast compound. The command vessel, from which Imnitrin had directed the battle, settled on a knoll overlooking the crowd. Around it was a dense ring of Rotrox soldiers.

"Are you really going to let these men go home with Blue Space?" I asked.

Imnitrin looked at me, his eyebrows lifted. "These are the more rebellious spirits of Rheatt. They will be a source of trouble while they live. A promise made to an enemy is not a promise."

He gave a signal to an officer through the open side of the cylinder. The ring of soldiers opened fire into the dense mass with their flame-lances. The disarmed prisoners surged to and fro, screaming and groaning.

The mass murder went on apace, bringing an increasing stench of burned flesh.

I looked questioningly at Bec. He shrugged. So I didn't think any more about it.

At the back of my mind I knew we were destroying a beautiful, delicate culture for a vicious, unbeautiful one. But my upbringing and experience had taught me full well that beauty and delicacy are not what count. Force and effectiveness were what counted.

Ten

"Don't be fooled by the Rotrox, Klein. They're technically proficient savages, that's all. They're tribal, like the Killibol nomads, not city-dwellers like us."

I had been expressing my concern at the speed with which Bec had been pushing himself in his position in the new Administration of Rheatt. The Rotrox, I thought, would resent the way he was taking matters into his own hands and running things the way they should be run.

"They look city-style to me," I replied.

"Nah. That's because they're disciplined and like pushing people around. These covered mazes they build look impressive but in essence they're only like the earthen warrens those little animals out on the plain dig. They wouldn't have a clue how to organise a complex city like Klittmann; they don't even understand factory organisation. Take it from me, Klein, in the Basement they'd be punks, third-raters."

A Rheattite secretary placed another scroll in front of him. It was covered with the flowing native writing, which Bec wasn't proficient in yet. The secretary read it out to him while he followed the text as best he could. Finally he nodded and stamped his seal on it with a thump.

"Oh, they've got the ideas," he continued, "they just haven't got the experience. You see, up on Merame they have a natural tribal obedience. Every young Rotrox is trained to accept the tribal order and to put his nation before everything else. They make war with other tribes, but apart from that there's little conflict. No internal tension. Consequently they haven't sharpened their wits on one another the way we have." He chuckled. "Imnitrin wouldn't last five minutes on Mud Street. Even here in Rheatt they were floundering. Believe me, we're the best thing that could have happened to them, and they know it."

Maybe Bec's right, I thought. The Rotrox idea of empire was a submissive population and massive tribute in raw materials, goods and slaves. But having once destroyed Rheatt's will, they hadn't known how to ensure that their orders were carried out. Bec had leaped instantly into this vacuum.

The Rheattite secretary left the room. He hadn't been able to read the document too easily, either, because the light in Bec's office was kept low enough to be comfortable for us Klittmannites without the use of dark goggles.

I had just returned from setting up a small factory about fifty miles away. It was the first of many such projects Bec had in mind. This one was only meant to turn out ammunition for our Hackers, Jains and smaller repeaters. In a few weeks the sloop would be fully operational again.

The Rheattites were new to the idea of factory production. They did everything on a one-off, artisan basis. But I was satisfied I had done a good enough job with the resources available. Things would really get rolling once we set up the production of machine tools. Bec had promised the Rotrox Jains and Hackers of their own.

Harmen was still down there, supervising quality control. His services had been invaluable: his technical knowledge was greater than anybody else's. I wasn't even sure what the HE formula was for the cartridges and shells, for instance. The old alk wasn't really interested in our schemes, of course, but Bec always managed to persuade him to co-operate somehow.

Apart from Harmen's technical expertise, Bec and I were on our own. Grale, Reeth and Hassmann had taken the sloop back to Blue Space Valley. Their presence there, Bec pointed out, would still be our trump card for some time to come.

"I don't know why," I said, "but it just gives me a funny feeling to be giving orders to these big Meramites. I wouldn't like it if I was them."

Bec shrugged. "They don't see it that way. Ostensibly I'm not the boss around here yet. Imnitrin's the governor and we're take orders; and we're acting in Imnitrin's name, not our own.

Later, when we come into our own, then we might have trouble. But we'll handle it."

He bent over some of his private notes. "Right now our main problem is to give the Rheattites some feeling of stability. Now they're getting Blue Space again they might get an upsurge of rebelliousness and Imnitrin will start trampling on them again. That will only set us back."

"Imnitrin has demanded a million slaves right away. Can't we persuade him to cut down that figure?"

"He wouldn't understand. Besides, his masters on Merame are impatient to see the Rotrox tribe become a race of warriors who don't have to work for their living. We'll get the million by transporting entire communities from outlying districts. That way it won't be noticed so much. We can always put around the idea that anybody sent to Merame is going to come back after a term of service."

"Who's going to swallow that?" I wanted to know.

"Don't be hasty; maybe we can even arrange it in time. All the Rotrox care about is results. They like success when they see it, and that's what we're giving them."

"I never thought I'd see you soft-pedalling anybody," I said, grinning.

Bec smiled tightly. "I learned quite a lot from those old books Tone got from Harmen. They called it "statecraft": the art of manipulating society. You know something, Klein? I think I like it here. There's room to manoeuvre. Klittmann was like being in a pressure chamber!" He laughed. "Anyway, that brings me to another matter I want you to attend to."

He paused. "I've found out something interesting. It seems the Rheattites had a National Leader called Dalgo, who got wiped out during the first wave of the Rotrox assault. His wife's still alive and living here right under our noses. Apparently she's still something of a symbolic figure for the Rheattites. She could exert a lot of influence."

"Why haven't the Rotrox killed her?" I asked.

He frowned. "You'd expect them to, wouldn't you? Anyway, go and see her, Klein. Maybe we can make some use of her."

The Lady Palramara lived in one of the green towers that

dotted the capital plain of Rheatt — the Rheattites called the place by a name that meant simply "parkland". By now the Rotrox corridors had overgrown Parkland, tentacling out and trampling down its beautiful gardens, squeezing it tight like some monster.

The Rotrox always preferred to build an enclosed corridor rather than an open road. My Rotrox driver took me in my private runabout through the maze of corridors. We came out by a side exit and there, a short distance away over the springy turf, was the tower, rising tall and slender for about a hundred feet.

I told the driver to wait and walked to the oval doorway at the base of the tower. Inside, it was all green shadow. I stepped in and felt myself being lifted up, passing through a confusion of light and shade, all green. Shortly the elevator came to a stop and a panel slid aside.

"Please enter," a cool, musical voice said. "I have been told to expect you."

I walked slowly into the room at the top of the green tower. It was the most beautiful room I had ever seen. It was not large, yet it gave an impression of spaciousness and airiness. The contours were all rounded, the windows broad and graceful. The walls were a pale green. The furniture and ornaments were of a darker green and of a light, glowing mauve which matched the eyes of the woman standing there.

The room I saw only in a secondary, incidental way. My eyes locked immediately on the Lady Palramara.

All Rheattite women are graceful; but she was graceful and something else with it. She didn't run to skinniness like a lot of her countrywomen: her green flesh was full and round, and soft. Her face was gentle and kind, with stunning liquid eyes, the pupils wide from heavy use of Blue Space.

Straight away you knew she had containment: self-reliance. She was sad, but not beaten. The flowing mauve gown she wore accentuated her curves and made you notice every movement.

"You are one of the men from the unknown world, are you not?" she asked calmly. "Servants of the Rotrox?"

I tore my eyes away from her to case the room. You couldn't put assassination past someone in her position, especially as she was a woman. I'd come across women carrying a gun for some guy before. I stepped to the window and peered out at the landscape with its odd mixure of Rheattite and Rotrox architecture.

"The light is bright for you?" she asked. "I have heard about your sensitivity. Perhaps I can be more hospitable. . . ."

She moved to a table and did something there. The window panes suddenly shimmered and took on a sepia cast. The room was only slightly dimmer, but the quality of the light had changed somehow. I risked lifting my goggles and found that I could see without discomfort.

"Is that convenient?" she asked. "The light is adequate for me also at this level. It is a matter of selecting the right frequencies."

I smiled at her, putting the goggles in my pocket. "That's a neat trick."

"Merely one more aid to creating a pleasant mode of living." She moved to the other side of the room as if to get a better look at me, leaning back and resting her hands on a ledge.

"That matters a lot to you people, doesn't it?" I said. "Making beautiful surroundings. Making life beautiful."

"Better than conquest and domination. Unfortunately some qualities are always developed at the expense of others. We failed to defend ourselves against the ravages of the Rotrox. What is it you want with me?"

"I'll be frank, Lady. Rheatt is conquered and you'll just have to accept that. But we might be able to make things a lot easier on your people than they would otherwise be. I'm not too fond of the Rotrox myself, but we have to co-operate with them for reasons of our own. We don't want to see your way of life destroyed if we can avoid it. According to what we hear you're still a person who commands respect in Rheatt. Maybe you could help us. We could give you some official position. It would help the people feel safe again. In return you could help us put through the programme we want."

"You think the Rotrox would allow that?" she said sharply.

"I believe so. They've accepted everything else we've suggested."

"You misunderstand. A woman does not hold official positions in Rheatt, or on Merame. My influence, if I have any, is not of that kind. I cannot take my husband's place, especially while he still lives."

I raised my eyebrows in surprise. "I thought your husband was killed at the outset of the war?"

Her liquid eyes seemed to look through me. Then she turned away, gazing through the wide windows. I wondered if she was always as charged on Blue Space as she seemed to be right now. The drug had the property of turning even tragedy into a poetic experience. I reflected that she was probably making things bearable for herself that way.

She began to speak in a low, detached voice. "They came at the beginning of summer. For us, it was a summer war. Big cylinders of aluminium and copper descending from the sky, shining in the sun. What was there for me to do? You clearly do not understand a woman's role on our world. I stayed here in this room, rearranging the ornaments on successive days to create pleasing variety, as was the custom. Outside, through this window, I saw my husband's aircraft crash to the ground."

"But he didn't die?"

"Many believe him to be dead, but he survived, though injured. The Rotrox dragged him from the wreck and took him to Merame, where they keep him prisoner. Once every thirty days they show him to me on television, though he does not know it." She gestured to a circular screen in the corner. "Sometimes they torture him before my eyes."

"And you watch?" I said, amazed.

"What should I do? If I do not watch, it takes place just the same. The Rotrox by tradition are not kind to the defeated. If you want to help me, make them release my husband."

I shook my head dumbly. "I don't think I can arrange that. He's the National Leader."

"No, of course you cannot." She looked at me again in a glazed, gentle way. "You see how helpless I am. I hope you will make life easier for Rheatt, but you see that I cannot help you."

So that seemed to be all there was to it. I didn't want to leave that room, but I couldn't think of a good excuse for staying. Reluctantly I made to go.

At the door she stopped me. "Nevertheless your . . . plans

interest me. If you want to bring me news or if you have questions, you are welcome."

Something in me quickened as I heard the invitation. I nodded, and left.

I couldn't get the Rheattite woman off my mind. All the women I'd known in Klittmann had been hard and brittle. She was different: she had qualities I hadn't met in women before.

I did go back. Then I started visiting her regularly. We talked for hours on end. I told her all about Klittmann and how we had come to arrive on Earth. But I never talked much about Becmath; the tool doesn't want to talk about the hand that guides it.

In return she talked about her life before the Rotrox came. It sounded real good: easy, pleasant and fulfilling, with none of the strain and neurotic striving of Klittmann. I guess I wouldn't have fitted in there — I was too set in my attitude to turn soft now — but just the same the time I spent up in that beautiful green room came to be the best part of the day.

For a long time I didn't touch her. I'm not sure why — there was nobody to stop me and nobody she could have complained to. It's just that it was a new experience being with a woman like her. But often she was blocked almost out of her mind with Blue Space and my chance came.

She was taking the stuff more and more heavily. I knew she was way over the norm: most people just took it occasionally. One night she passed out in mid-sentence. I picked her up off the floor. The blood surged through me as I held her there in my arms. I carried her down some recessed steps into a bedchamber below the main room.

I knew she would be all right. Blue Space didn't do anybody any real harm. I laid her down on the sleeping couch. She stirred and opened her eyes, staring up at me with big, sleepy eyes. I realised she wouldn't really be aware of who I was, that she might even confuse me with her husband. I struggled with the temptation for a moment, then gave way to my urges.

I sank down on her, falling into a soft, warm bed of delight.

When I told Bec that the National Leader was still alive on Merame he listened to me, shaking his head with incredulity, and said: "Those klugs certainly know how to be vindictive."

Later he asked me where I was getting to in the evenings, so I told him.

He stroked his chin. "And the old man's up on Merame, eh? Tell you what, Klein, how would you like me to get Imnitrin to put a bullet in him for you?"

I had known how far my feelings for Palramara were going when I had started hoping that word would come through that that poor klug, Dalgo, would turn up dead. "It sounds like a good idea," I said immediately. But my voice was weak.

"Of course, he'll probably make it something slower. It's traditional." Bec meaningfully scratched his side where the pincers had bitten into his flesh.

I didn't speak for a long moment. "Let it go, Bec," I said eventually. "Do me a favour. Leave things as they are."

"Sure, Klein. Anything you say."

He didn't refer to it again. We were pretty busy setting up organisations staffed mostly by Rheattites with some token supervision by Meramites; though the big grey men didn't actually do very much. We had pulled Reeth out of Blue Space Valley to help train Rheattite technicians to make Klittmann-type armaments. Already we had a workshop-style pilot scheme going. Now we were ready to expand into what would eventually be a full-scale factory.

Bec was convinced that once guns started rolling off the production line and into Rotrox hands we would finally have gained their full confidence. Any suspicions they might still have about our intentions would be dispelled; and even better, we could jointly set a tentative date for the invasion of Killibol — which was the Big Thing Bec was aiming at.

Already Bec tended to stay more and more in his office, sending me out to do the spadework. I gained a wealth of experience that way. As usual Bec was quick to latch on to technical gimmicks and he was setting up a television network that enabled him to watch practically everything in Rheatt.

Wherever I went Bec's television face was there to give me guidance.

Setting up the factory was a big job. Bec sent me out to supervise all of it, with Reeth and Harmen. The place was to be guarded by Rotrox warriors to ensure that none of the products got into the wrong hands, and otherwise was to be managed solely by Rheattite technicians, members of the new élite that Bec planned for the Rheattic nation. The factory was about fifty miles away from Parkland. I spent about four weeks there getting things running smoothly and sorting out the discipline a factory needs. At the end of it the Rheattites had begun to cotton on, but I was exhausted.

When I arrived back in Parkland Bec wasn't in his quarters. I went straight over to Palramara's tower, more than ready to relax in my favourite location on the planet Earth. The elevator took me smoothly up through green shadows, like passing through water. I stepped into the room with the big windows.

Bec was there, lounging on a couch under one of the windows. He was naked to the waist: his shirt and boots were strewn across the other end of the room. Palramara was there, too. She had seen me come in but she didn't look at me, simply turned away and gazed out of the window.

The situation was spelled out clearly enough. It didn't need any speeches. "How long have you been here?" I demanded bluntly.

"Just a couple of weeks, on and off. Ever since I decided to take a look at this dame." Bec scratched his hairy chest. "I found out why the Rotrox didn't bump her off, Klein. It seems they have a tradition: the conqueror gets the use of the conquered chieftain's wife. Cute, isn't it? Naturally, Imnitrin doesn't care for Earth females so he just let her be."

"And why should that bring *you* in?" I said harshly.

"Why, I've got Imnitrin's job now. You did a fine job on the factory, Klein. When the Hackers started rolling off the production line Imnitrin took the first batch home to Merame to show the Tribal Council. He never liked it much on Earth anyway and he persuaded them to appoint me Governor in his place. So the tradition devolves on me. I have to do my duty now I'm practically a member of the Council of the Rotrox."

"Oh, sure," I sneered. "You were always big on tradition, weren't you?"

Bec smiled unpleasantly. "She's not too badly off. Look at it this way, she could have got Imnitrin." Unconcernedly he drank from a goblet. "O.K., Klein, I'll see you in the morning. Be at the office early, we've a lot of work on hand."

The blood seemed to be drumming in my head. The gun in my holster was itching to leap into my hand. If it had been anybody else, Grale or even Reeth, I would have shot him down without a thought. As it was I was paralysed. I stood there glaring. Then without another word I walked out.

I reported early next morning, just as Bec said. He was already there. He nodded to me as I came in. The television screens that lined one wall of his office were all alive, mostly showing deserted scenes in various parts of Rheatt and at the new factory; we hadn't inaugurated a night shift yet.

"Klein," he said, "I've been thinking we ought to set up a training school for young Rheattites—"

"Cut it out," I interrupted. "Find another whipping-boy, I've quit."

He looked at me sourly. "You're quitting, Klein? Where're you gonna quit to?"

"I'll worry about that. This is just to tell you. Maybe Grale's more your man anyway."

"Maybe he is at that. He'd know better than to lose his head over a woman."

I looked him straight in the eye. I knew he could feel my hatred. "You did it on purpose, didn't you?" I accused.

"What is it you want? Girls? You can have all the girls you want. I'll get you plenty. You can have anything you want here in Rheatt, provided it's only a one-way trade. You're too important to me to let anything go worming into your guts. I need your undivided energy, and that means nobody goes changing your mind about anything or turns you soft."

"Who's going soft?" I challenged.

He snorted softly. "The Klein I first knew in Klittmann would have had Dalgo bumped off without a qualm. I knew then that you had something else besides our Big Project on your mind."

"Project?"

"You know what I mean. What we're doing here in Rheatt is only our platform for the real operation. Neither Rheatt nor the Rotrox are of much interest to me: they don't have the right qualities, they're weak punks, klugs. Killibol's the world, the world we're going to transform. It's like a bomb waiting to be let off. We're going to release all the energies pent up in those cities. We'll make a society, an empire, where almost anything will be possible. . . ."

His oddly glittering eyes met my sullen stare, meeting the hatred and beating it down. He seemed to know that I found this vision of his irresistible. It was the idea of working for something bigger than yourself, something that would outlast you and be permanent. Bec also knew that I was the only one of the mob who understood this idea.

"It has to be this way, Klein," he said. "It's a matter of destiny. If you want a part in it then you have to belong to me, not to that woman in the tower. It's too big a job for that, I don't want any emotional entanglements. You can have girls *but they can't have you*. Have fun, but your feelings can go in only one direction."

"Did you have to do it this way?" I said, still surly.

"Why not, it's as good as any other. Don't tell me you're going to fold up like a sack of water?" He gazed at me curiously. "It's a funny thing, you get guys who are brave in the face of bullets, grenades, cops, anything you can name, but they haven't got what it takes when something hits them in the gut like this. Don't tell me you're one of those hollow men. I hope I know character better than that."

"I can take it."

"I thought so." Bec was silent for a moment. Then he cocked his head, looking at me slyly. "Tell you what I'll do, Klein. You can have the woman back. Go on, take her. Only you'll be out of it, like you just said. You'll have quit. You'll live out your life here in Rheatt and nobody will bother you, I'll do the job on my own. Nothing can stop me now, anyway."

I gave a deep sigh. "You know me better than that."

"I think so."

For a moment he looked at me with what might have been sympathy. I remembered Gelbore, the girl on the raft with us.

I wondered when Bec was going to stop making emotional demands of me.

I didn't try to see Palramara after that. Bec, however, continued visiting her regularly.

Eleven

I had just woken up when the gentle tone sounded. Becmath's face came up in monochrome on the television screen, which was muted to suit Klittmann eyes.

He was frowning. "Can you get over here, Klein? There's something needs attending to straight away."

"I'll be with you," I said, and the image faded.

I dressed quickly, wondering what was up. I hadn't seen Bec in the flesh for over half a year.

We'd been in operation now for something like four years. Everything had gone fairly smoothly, barring a few wrinkles here and there. The production lines were now turning out weapons, aircraft, and a modified version of the sloop. About fifty per cent of everything we made went to Merame, as well as masses of other manufactured goods and raw materials.

Rheatt was still garrisoned by Rotrox troops, but everything was quiet and their numbers grew less every year. Bec had recruited an élite organisation from among Rheattite youngsters who had never taken Blue Space, given them training in arms, concocted an ideology and indoctrinated them with it. They were contemptuous of the life styles of their parents and looked on Bec almost as a god.

Bec had done all this without so far arousing the opposition of the Council of the Rotrox. He had even persuaded them to put off their conquests of other Earth nations and continents until sufficient stocks of the new weapons had been built up.

The fact that Rheatt was running like a well-oiled machine was due entirely to Bec's master-planning, with a little help from me and the boys. It didn't alter the fact that we, the new masters of this country, were essentially mobsters and still thought and acted like mobsters.

We must have seemed strange, remote figures to the Rheat-tite population. Once things settled down we had become recluse, living in green towers dotted about the landscape. Grale and Hassmann shared a tower, otherwise each of us had had his own tower built, lacking windows and completely cut off from the outside world, where we each lived according to his own propensities. Reeth had designed the inside of his dwelling himself and had covered the walls with paintings of naked Killibollian women he had somehow got a local artist to paint from imagination. He had a different Rheattite woman every day. Tone the Taker's place was simply a den where he kept himself in a permanently drugged condition. Harmen, apart from his private dwelling, also staffed an alchemical laboratory with about twenty Rheattite assistants. Currently, so I heard, he was trying to get a nuclear reactor built.

I had purposefully built my own tower without too much luxury. Unlike the others, who had nothing but leisure on their hands, there was still plenty for me to do. I was Bec's liaison for the armaments programme and for training the League of Rheatt, as the youth organisation was called. Bec himself never went out now, and every day he called me on the screen for conferences and instructions.

Dressed and armed, I checked the outside. Bright light filtered through the screen of cloth I used to do this, momentarily lighting up the interior with a green glow. I judged it was mid-afternoon, took the elevator down and put on my dark goggles while I drove over to Bec's tower.

The elevator took me in automatically. Bec was seated in a deep soft chair, a glass of *hwura,* an intoxicating beverage, in his hand. In Klittmann he had smoked a lot of weed, but now we couldn't get that he drank *hwura* instead.

Bec was almost surrounded by television screens and piles of documents and written reports.

"Hello, Klein," he said. "I think somebody's trying to do a takeover. Come and look at this."

Several of the screens were alive. Only as I crossed the room did I see the one he was watching. It showed a number of Rotrox leaning over something. When one of them moved I could see that what they were leaning over was Tone the Taker. He was lying on his back on a couch, his features vacant. Their voices came over, blurred and indistinguishable. I strained my ears but could make out nothing.

"They've been trying to get Tone to tell them where the gateway to Killibol is," Bec supplied.

"Has he told them?"

"No, but only because he's too blocked to know what's going on. When he needs another shot he'll start to come round and then he'll tell them anything."

"Why do they want to know? Is Imnitrin trying to bypass us?"

Bec shook his head. "I don't think so. I've been hearing vague rumblings for some time. There's always been a small caucus on Merame that resented our influence and our reconstituting the Rheattic nation instead of destroying it completely. Evidently this is an action group. Their idea will be to seize the gateway, probe beyond it, and if it looks good try to gain enough support for a wholly Rotrox invasion. At the same time they'll want us shouldered out."

I stared at the scene. One of the Rotrox was shaking Tone. "Isn't that somewhat rebellious? Could they pull it off? What would the Council think?"

Bec moved uneasily. "It's a funny thing about the Rotrox. I've noticed that an idea or an argument can be in the air for years without anything happening. The Council might even veto it. But if somebody takes some action on their own and it begins to look as if it's moving, they get interested. Consequently I don't want these zealots poking into our business. Especially, I don't want them poking around on Killibol."

"Why not? They'd simply find a dead world."

"That's why it would be so bad. They could convince the Council that I've been lying to them. The Rotrox are expecting all kinds of loot out of Killibol."

There was one other question I wanted to ask.

"Have you got all our towers bugged?"

"Between you and me — no. Only Tone's and Harmen's. I figured that would only be sensible."

"It looks like you were right. What do you want me to do about this?"

"Take a squad over there and don't leave anybody alive."

"Isn't that a bit drastic?" I asked. "The Rotrox might not like that."

"I'll square it. They're not squeamish about expending their young bloods. I'll make it look like they came in shooting and Tone's bodyguard defended him. That might convince the action caucus that we're more solidly entrenched than they thought we were."

"Right."

As I turned to go, Bec added: "By the way, when I said leave nobody alive I meant nobody. And that goes for Tone, too."

I paused. "Is that necessary?" I said. "He is one of us."

"He's the only weak link in the chain and I want him out of the way. They wouldn't dare to try this on any of the others. I seem to remember you missed Tone once before. Now's your chance to make up for it."

Tone's tower was nearly two hundred miles away. I rustled up a well-armed squad of ten young Rheattites and we commandeered a fast aircraft from a nearby airfield. It could do well over four hundred miles per hour fully loaded, and we weren't long in getting there.

Bec had told me he had counted five Rotrox in the tower, but there could well have been more. Also, they might have heard the noise of the motor as we approached. I studied the tower from behind a grove of trees, reflecting on how well that type of building was suited to withstand an assault.

However long you looked at it there was only one thing to do and that was to go in through the main entrance at ground level. By now it was evening; the sun was below the horizon and I could dispense with my eye filters. Cool, fresh perfumes drifted across the ground from the trees, grass and flowers. The squad knew its business; I gave the command and across the open ground we went, my men moving quick and lithe in their cat-suit uniforms.

We made it to the base of the tower and found the elevator empty and intact. I left three men outside and the rest of us surged upward in the confined space. In those few seconds, I knew, we were extremely vulnerable. I stopped the elevator two floors below Tone's living quarters.

We piled out into dark, silent and empty rooms. Tone had built the fat tower much larger than his requirements. Probably without even knowing it. I led the way up staircases until we came to the occupied storey which was lit and furnished.

The first spacious room we went through, though unoccupied, bore evidence of Tone's hobby. The furnishings were streamlined and sparse. The whole room was in blue (Earth sky-blue) and the walls were taken up with giant television screens which crawled with eye-dizzying patterns in various shades of blue.

A murmur of clipped, high-pitched Rotrox voices came from the next room. I signalled the Rheattites to move quietly. We crossed the floor to the wide doors with their hand-carved friezes. I kicked it open and we burst through.

The scene was more or less as I had seen it on the television screen in Bec's tower. The Rotrox stood around the supine Tone, talking among themselves and waiting for him to recover consciousness sufficiently to put himself in their power.

Our repeaters blasted out without warning. The Rotrox had time to turn, to reach for their weapons, then they were skittering across the room under the impact of a hail of lead, tumbling over the furniture.

In seconds the deafening violence was over. I checked the bodies to make sure they were dead. From what I could see, Tone hadn't been touched. I decided I had better do the next part of the job alone.

"Get back downstairs and wait for me at the base of the tower,' I ordered. They left. I looked close at Tone. His eyes were closed.

Then it struck me. There were four dead Rotrox in the room. Bec had mentioned five. There had to be another one somewhere in the tower.

There was another door at the opposite end of the room. I sidled to it, eased it open, and slipped inside. It was another blue room. In the one or two seconds that I cased it the fifth Rotrox entered by a door to my right.

We saw each other in the same moment. In his hand he had one of the short-bladed swords the Rotrox usually carried. Apparently he had no firearm. I brought up my repeater and nipped back the trigger.

And the repeater jammed.

Mentally I cursed. The repeater was Rheatt-made — despite all our efforts Rheattite workmanship still didn't measure up to the home version. My mind leaped immediately to the handgun in my inside holster and to the guns the dead Rotrox had carried in the other room, but there was no time to do anything about either. The Rotrox came at me in a flash, sword extended, and I had just a split second to save my life.

His limbs *chink-chinked* as he sprang at me. Four years ago it had taken me quite a while to find out what the movable rod-like arrangement was on Rotrox legs and arms. Merame is only one-sixth the size of Earth or Killibol and its gravity is correspondingly less. The silvery rods and pistons were assists: motorised extra muscles without which the Rotrox could scarcely stand up in Earth's heavy gravity.

I hurled myself aside, just managing to dodge his sword thrust. As his grinning grey face swept past me I took my repeater by the barrel and swung the stock at his nearside calf, smashing the rod arrangement where it junctioned with the ankle. There was a tinkling noise. The Rotrox fell heavily to the floor as his leg collapsed under him. He floundered there, trying to raise himself with his arms and his good leg. That gave me the moment I needed to draw my handgun and shoot him through the head.

I listened for any further sound in the building. There was none. I went back to where Tone lay on the couch. His eyes were open, now. He looked up at me, his pupils huge.

"They wanted information," he said dreamily, his voice faint. "I held back. I've been awake for some time."

The gun was still in my hand. When he saw it there, the way it was pointing, he seemed to guess what was going to happen.

"I'm a risk, aren't I?" he said, struggling to a half-sitting position. "I'm not in control of myself."

"We have to protect ourselves" I said stonily.

"Sure." He stared, glazed, up into my face. "Shoot me, Klein. Go on, shoot me. Then I'll be free, floating in Blue Space forever."

I levelled the gun. Suddenly his face twisted wryly.

"Becmath's hatchet-man!"

The blast sounded incongruously loud. The slug made a

neat hole in his face and blew a chunk out of the back of his skull. He jerked back on to the couch, dead before he even knew it.

Quickly and efficiently I went through the other rooms to make sure there was no one else and then rejoined the squad. I wondered if Bec, watching in his tower two hundred miles away, had picked up Tone's last remark.

Twelve

The planet Earth spins in a space filled with brilliant light. The atmosphere glows with the brightness of it. On that planet, the country of Rheatt is like one vast jewel glowing with colours, a big bowl of green grass and heady scents from the drooping trees.

Sometimes, from within my tower, I would peep at the spectacle of the setting or rising sun throwing vivid colours across the sky. Alien though it was, I could see the beauty of it.

Nine years had passed since we had first broken through the gateway from Killibol. Nine years in which we, the masters of Rheatt, had lurked invisibly in our sealed towers, rarely seen by the natives or by each other. Rheatt answered to our commands because we had organised it that way. Millions of Rheattites worked on Merame in Rotrox workshops or as household slaves. Down on Earth they manned the factories that, slowly but surely, had been turning out the weapons to equip an army. The muscles and nerves of the new order in Rheatt were supplied by a military-style élite that had never known Blue Space. They had been trained by us personally. They had their own kind of toughness, even of brutality, and they were in awe of the white men who had achieved all this.

There were still Rotrox in Rheatt, too, stalking about with their habitual arrogance, sometimes with the traditional molten metal-spewing lances, but more often with the repeaters and handguns that we had given them. They were respected by the Rheattic élite, but not admired.

Mine was the face that was most known in Rheatt. The organisation was largely my direct handiwork, and I still put in a personal appearance from time to time. But lately, like the others, I had grown taciturn and had withdrawn into a self-created environment.

Becmath had not stepped outside his tower for years. I myself had not seen him in the flesh since I had killed Tone; but he had been there, the constant shadow that followed and instructed me by television.

So it was something of an event when Bec called us together. When I entered his apartment Reeth, Grale and Hassmann were already there, sitting around waiting for me. Bec was sitting in the same chair that I had seen him in five years before, still surrounded by flickering television screens.

Of us all, Bec had aged the most. His white face had become slightly puffy and his eyes were tired. The others were simply ten years older, but fit and alert. At that, though, Bec was the only one who hadn't put on weight through eating so much rich food.

He wasted no time in getting down to business.

"I guess you boys didn't believe me, that time when we were on the outside and running, that one day we'd be back to get even with all those klugs who crossed us," he said, "but that day has come. Now's the time for the push on Klittman."

Reeth shrugged. "I'm happy as things are. But anything you say, boss."

Grale grinned. His face had become more swarthy in the years we'd lived in Rheatt. "It can't be too soon for me. We've been too long in this damned sun-drenched, green-skinned place."

"That's the idea," Bec said approvingly. "You think we're doing all right here? So we are. But we're living on the wrong planet. Wait till we've finished on Killibol: Klittmann's only the beginning, we're going to move all over. I'll give you a city apiece all for your own. Ten cities apiece. Nobody knows just how many cities there are on Killibol."

"What about the Rotrox, Bec?" Hassmann rumbled. "Where do they fit in?"

Bec snorted, making a vague gesture with his hand. "They'll expect it to be their empire, like Rheatt. But don't worry: I don't intend to be their hireling for very long. In the cities of Killibol we'll be in a world they don't understand at all. Furthermore we'll have gigantic industries and the energies of trained populations all at our disposal. It'll make our effort here look like protein peanuts."

Grale gave a delighted laugh. "You mean we're gonna push those klugs out of it, boss? I like that!"

"That's right. We'll play along with them for a short while, but we'll soon push them off Killibol; and then we'll push them right off Rheatt and back up on to Merame. They can have Merame, I don't want it."

Reeth made a face. "What do we want with Rheatt, if it comes to that? Let them have it. We can guard the gateway and they'd never get through. We could even destroy it again."

"We'll need Rheatt for a while," Bec said without explanation.

I presumed he meant we'd need it for the sake of the Rheattite troops who would be on the campaign. He wouldn't want to throw away all the work we'd done here. At that, it would be some months, at least, before we were sufficiently consolidated in Klittmann to consider turning against our blood brothers, the Rotrox tribe.

I had kept silent so far because I already knew Bec's mind on these matters. Now he turned to me.

"We have to straighten out the position with the Rotrox, Klein. I want you to make a trip to Merame and talk to the Council."

A slight chill went up my spine at the thought of appearing before those cold, cruel men on their own ground.

"What do I tell them?"

"Formally it's a request from me for them to order the campaign and contribute their own forces. I'll give you a recorded message in my own voice. Besides that, we have to cover our rear. I don't want any funny business going on while we're all away in Klittmann settling scores. So make it look like we have a common accord and play the good servant."

Hassmann, Grale and Reeth were all grinning.

Grale clapped his hands together. "I've waited nine years to get my hands on some white women!"

I travelled in one of the cylinders that regularly dropped

out of the sky and ascended again to Merame. This was my first time off-planet — the first time for any of us.

The cylinders worked by acting on the Earth's magnetic field in some way, and they gave off a loud humming when they moved that reverberated through the crude, cavernous interior. Crossing between Earth and Merame was as much as they could manage: they were helpless deeper in inter-planetary space.

I would have liked to take a look at a deep space, but there weren't any windows. The crossing lasted about a day; then a heavy jolt told me we had landed on Merame.

The Rotrox crew gladly stripped off their muscle assists. They were in their own element now.

A section of the wall opened up to form a ramp. The cold, thin air of Merame breezed in.

The sun was on the horizon, looking small and hot. The landscape was dull and grey, the soil lead-like. Some stunted, scrubby-looking bushes grew here and there, looking poor and wretched and cowed by the sharply rising mountains to the south.

At one time, according to Harmen, Merame had possessed neither life nor air. It was habitable now only because of the work of man, who either by accident or design had intro-duced species which had survived and adapted themselves gradually to local conditions, like the Meramites themselves. Plants and bacteria had released an atmosphere out of the soil and in the course of time a self-supporting ecology had developed.

Neither the Earth nor the Meramite races were aware of this. It had all happened a million years ago, back before the dawn of their history.

The Rheattite secretary I had brought with me to help with the language scanned the scene. I could see the revulsion writ-ten on his face. To his cultured eyes the bleak landscape was like hell, an impression intensified by his already having served a spell here as a slave.

But I found that I quite liked it. It reminded me of Killibol, except that the light was still far too bright. Half a mile away some low hut-like structures were the only sign of human life. Our Rotrox guides stepped down the ramp and led the way.

Gone was the half-stalking, half-loping gait that had charac-
terised them on Earth: their tall, gangling, broad-chested
bodies really were adapted to low gravity and they walked upright with a new confidence.

My Rheattite had already advised me how I should walk:
body leaning forward slightly, taking small gliding steps, and
always thinking one step ahead. I got the hang of it after a
few yards and was able to continue looking around.

There was one other feature of Merame that gave it an even
closer, though bizarre, resemblance to Killibol. Dotted about
the landscape were lumpy monoliths of a rough, concrete-
like substance, looking for all the world like scale models of
Killibol cities.

But these were built by a species of insect called termites.
I had seen these rocky towers on Earth also, where they rarely
reached more than about seven feet in height. The Merame
termites had evolved to a size of three or four inches and their
silent, rocky pillars rose between fifty and a hundred feet.

We passed through the shadow of one of them to reach the
Rotrox buildings. These turned out to be more extensive than
had appeared at first, forming a barrack-like circle round the
rim of a large crater whose further end was lost in darkness.
The lip of the crater had been smoothed down to the level of
the surrounding terrain and its floor, about a hundred feet
below us, was lost in shadows and flickering, purple lights.

We entered one of the buildings, which was similar to the
corridor-like structures I was used to on Earth, and which had
open doors in each wall through which I glimpsed the crater
down below. Our Rotrox guides spoke to an older countryman
who wore, in addition to the tribal uniform, a long flaring
cloak, and then withdrew. The elderly Rotrox stared at me,
ignoring the Rheattite, and gave a cold, withering smile.

"Welcome to Merame, blood-brother. The Council of the
Rotrox knows of your arrival and will receive you now. Are
you prepared?"

Bec and I had both studied Rotrox, but not deeply. I could
just about follow him. The Rheattite interpreter, receiving no
signal from me, said nothing. I nodded.

He led us through the opposite door and on to a platform
which overhung the lip of the crater. The platform was an

elevator: we sank down into the gloom past a smooth wall lined with numerous entrances. It seemed the whole lining of the crater was riddled with tunnels.

The platform came to a halt at one of these. We walked along it for some distance in silence. It was lit by fierce electric lights which cast an eerie, slightly greenish radiance and made the skin of the Rotrox look as if it was covered in some sort of fungus. Finally he took us down a flight of spiral steps and into a circular chamber more luxurious than anything we had seen so far.

The Council of the Rotrox lounged on low couches, their long legs sprawled out over the floor. There were eight of them, including the man who had brought us here and who now took his place among them. They were arranged roughly in a semi-circle. Behind them blank-faced Rheattite slaves stood on attendance.

Rotrox faces all look alike to me, but I recognised Imnitrin by the duelling scar that ran across his brow and down his left cheek. He nodded a greeting to me, climbed to his feet and named the others in turn.

The Rotrox language is poor in vowels; it has only two: short *i* and short *o*, and it is rare for both to occur in the same word. The names of the rulers of Merame were: Oblo, Mincinitrix, Tinikimni, Koblorotovro, Oxotoblow, Villitrinimin and Ozhtoblorro. And, of course, Imnitrin. Rotrox speech was a train of almost indistinguishably like-sounding syllables, which made it difficult to learn.

Imnitrin sat down. I felt nervous with their eyes all on me, but I decided to waste no time. Speaking through the interpreter, I said: "I have a message, blood-brothers, from your servant Becmath, Governor of Rheatt."

Placing the recording on a table — which was Rotrox-size and came up to my chest — I flipped the switch. Bec's baritone voice came out, speaking Rotrox with studied ease.

"From the Governor of the territory of Rheatt to the Supreme Council of the Rotrox, rulers of all Merame and of Territories on Earth," Bec began. "I can now report to my blood-brothers that preparations are nearing completion for a successful conquest of the world of Killibol. I can promise my blood-brothers that if they so command the invasion can commence almost immediately, with every assurance of success. It is my fervent hope that the warriors of the Rotrox will be eager to join me in this great adventure."

The recording finished. One of the Rotrox — I had failed to keep track of their names — lifted up a Klittmann-type repeater that was lying on his couch.

"Our brother speaks of success. But are these not the weapons wielded also by the nations of Killibol? Could they not put millions of men in the field?"

"The people of Killibol live in large, enclosed cities which do not make war on one another," I explained. "They expect no attack and maintain no armies. There will be fighting, but with the help of one, perhaps two legions of Rotrox as well as the trained men of Rheatt who are now loyal to the Rotrox Empire, we cannot fail."

For a moment or two the iciness in the air made me think that something was wrong. But then the atmosphere suddenly broke. Imnitrin gestured imperiously to his green-skinned servant, who hurried forward and poured a dark musk-coloured fluid from a jug into a silver goblet, which he handed to me. I sipped the drink. It had a deep, earthy flavour.

"Tell Becmath that we are well pleased with our blood-brothers the white men of Killibol," said an aged Rotrox whose name might have been Oblo. "We shall despatch two legions to Earth for despatch to the new planet. Soon there will be three worlds in the Empire of the Rotrox and all beings everywhere will fear and quake at the mention of our name."

A feeling of relief passed through me. They suspected nothing of our long-term intentions. They were going to play along, although frankly I would have been happier with one legion rather than two of Rotrox rampaging about Klittmann. All those cold-minded warriors might be hard to handle, I thought.

They all tossed off their drinks and had them refilled. They were developing a kind of jovial camaraderie at the prospect of the coming campaign. Imnitrin promised he would command the two Rotrox legions himself.

"It will be a pleasure to fight alongside Becmath again," he said, his high-pitched voice becoming congratulatory and, perhaps, slightly drunk.

"Tell me," he continued, drinking yet more of the brew, "what will Becmath do with his enemies when he has them in his power?"

I shrugged. "Kill them, maybe, if they still oppose him."

"Kill them? That is a mild pleasure indeed." Imnitrin leaped to his feet. "Will he not punish them at length, taunt them and gloat over them? Where is the joy of conquest if it is not to see one's enemies miserable? Simply to die is no great pain. Come with me, brother, and perhaps Becmath will be interested to hear how *we* deal with the defeated."

He paused at the door and glanced at my Rheattite secretary. "Never mind your interpreter. I will speak Rheattite where necessary." The secretary, who had become more faltering and fearful as the councillors had become more jovial, thankfully joined his countrymen at the rear of the room.

Imnitrin led me through seemingly endless corridors and down winding stone steps. The atmosphere began to grow dank and depressing, the light dimmer. I sensed we were approaching the dungeons of this intricate warren.

"Let us through, jailer. Let the guest see our prisoners."

At the end of a corridor whose walls dripped moisture two Rotrox stood to attention before a vast metal door. With a jangling of chains and locks the door swung open. A faint cacophony of sighs, groans, mutterings and clinkings met my ears.

I got the impression that the dungeon was well ramified. Other corridors crossed the one we took. We sauntered down it, peering in cell after cell.

It was pretty sickening. The cells were mostly occupied by minor chiefs and notables from conquered tribes on Merame. The Rotrox were ingenious in thinking up unbearable circumstances for their victims to spend the rest of their lives in. Men — and sometimes women — wallowed in filth, in excrement. One stood up to his neck in water, another in a sort of mud that bubbled and gave off a thick stench and was intolerably hot. They hung from hooks or were entwined in intricate cutting machines that sliced their internal organs slowly and perpetually. They stared back at us with eyes long gone blank from prolonged suffering.

"Tell Becmath we will accommodate any special prisoners

he wishes to send us," Imnitrin piped cheerfully. "We can arrange special television coverage so that he can watch their agonies. Here is a prisoner of special interest to you — Dalgo, once chief of Rheatt. We have long grown bored with torturing him. We decided that he is most miserable when simply sitting in pitch darkness and brooding over the humiliation that has befallen his nation."

He flung open an iron door and flicked a switch, at which light flooded the darkened cell. The man who sat there at a small table looked up, dazzled.

So this was Dalgo. He was broad, for a Rheattite, and his face was less effete than was usual; it was a fighter's face. It was ravaged and lined by the time he had spent here in the Rotrox dungeons, yet somehow his shoulders were still straight and undefeated.

He said nothing. I stared at him, trying to imagine what it must have been like to have spent ten years in this place.

"I'd like to talk to him," I said suddenly.

Imnitrin smiled. "You wish to remind him of the situation? Good! He will not attack you; he has learned what that would mean to him. I will wait down the corridor."

He left, closing but not locking the door behind him.

"Who is there?" Dalgo said in a hollow voice. "The light hurts me."

"My name is Klein," I told him.

"Klein?" He seemed to be searching his mind for the name. "Ah, yes. Helper of Becmath, the Rotrox puppet who rules my country. They keep me informed, you see."

I wondered if we were being bugged. I hesitated, then said: "Have the Rotrox never offered you a deal? Maybe you could be useful to them. They might free you if you swear loyalty to them, like I did."

The faintest hint of a grim smile came to his lips. He turned his eyes away from the light. "I am giving them everything they want from me: pleasure at my discomfort. I have nothing else they need. I know that my country can never be freed from its oppression and for that reason alone they keep me alive. If I had hope, that would give them reason to kill me."

Wearily he passed his hand across his eyes. "Perhaps you serve them because you have no choice. I am their prisoner because *I* have no choice. There is no question of co-operation. They are no more than a blot on creation, but unfortunately the force does not exist that could expunge them."

"Your wife is still in Rheatt," I said after a pause.

He sighed. "Is she well?"

"Yes."

"She believes I am dead, I suppose."

"No," I told him. "She knows you're alive. The Rotrox saw to that."

A look of doggedness crossed his face. "Can you see her?"

"Yes, I think so."

"If you truly wish me well, tell her I am dead."

I could think of nothing else useful to say so I left, leaving the cell door open behind me. Up the corridor Imnitrin greeted me with the pinched-up, mincing expression of Rotrox hilarity.

"I confess I listened to your conversation via a hidden microphone," he piped. "My admiration for your cleverness increases apace. Your remarks were most ingenious. His mental anguish will intensify during the next few days as he relives the past." He gave a silvery snigger. "But come — we have prepared entertainments in your honour."

He took me out of the dungeon, through the maze of corridors that riddled the rock of Merame, and to one of the elevators that slid ceaselessly up and down the inner wall of the crater.

We sank to the bottom. No sunlight penetrated down here, though its horizontal rays could be seen flashing above. Through them, stars shone vividly like a carpet of gems in the sky. The crater floor was clothed in a kind of luminous gloom, and somewhere in the distance I could hear the muffled rattle of drums. Towards this sound we set off across the springy turf.

We walked for a good mile or more. A large number of buildings and fenced-off areas littered the crater floor: the Rotrox apparently used it as a recreation area. Shortly before we reached our destination I saw in one of the many glades a prime example of a stomach-churning Rotrox diversion.

On a piece of earth about fifty yards across, and fringed with drooping trees, a score or more of Rheattite people stood planted in the ground. That's right: planted people. It was obvious that they couldn't move their feet from where they were standing. Some were moaning, rocking gently to and fro; others wailed loudly, waving their arms imploringly at the sky.

Imnitrin smirked to see my amazement. "This is Tinikimni's Garden of the Vegetable People. I chanced to joke to him, one day, that as on Earth plants are green, so the green Rheattite people ought to be plants. It pleased Tinikimni's sense of the humorous to make a pleasant little spot stocked with such planted people. On to their feet are grafted composite animal-vegetable placentae which put down roots deep into the soil. From the soil they draw nutrients which they convert into blood. The blood is then infused through the plant-people's feet, giving them adequate nutrition. A pretty conceit, is it not? Quite inadvertently the transfusion process causes some agony, thus adding pain to their despair."

Imnitrin's understanding of me seemed to be that I could not fail to be amused and delighted by all this.

A few minutes later we came to a large compound where the dark liqueur the Rotrox drank flowed plentifully and warriors performed frenzied tribal dances to pulsing drums. For the first time since we had encountered the Rotrox I began to wonder what we had got into by teaming up with them and whether it was all worth it. I felt physically ill.

But what was I complaining about, I told myself? A mobster knows only one way of life and that is to find someone to intimidate, threaten and finally take a piece of. When we burst through to Earth we had gone ranging about like a torpedo, like parasites seeking a host or viruses seeking healthy gene machinery to take over and remake. We had found that host and it had worked for us, as Bec had always said it would: we had found the lever that moved vast forces in our favour. We were only doing what we had been doing all along, on a smaller scale, in Klittmann.

So what was bothering me?

Thirteen

The first thing I did on getting back to Rheatt, after reporting to Bec, was to go and see Palramara.

It had been a long time. The elevator took me up and I stepped into the once-familiar top room where she was waiting for me.

Rheattite women wear well: she hadn't changed much. "You wanted to see me," she said, sitting down and staring at me calmly.

Up to that point my mind hadn't been quite made up about whether to deliver Dalgo's message complete. I decided then that she deserved not to be told any lies. At the same time I realised that I could be brutal if I wanted. A part of me would have liked to hurt her because of what had happened. But I had to recognise that it hadn't been her fault: she had been a chattel, a spoil of war.

"I've been up on Merame," I told her. "I saw your husband. He asked me to give you a message."

Her eyes widened. "Yes?"

I hesitated. "Maybe I shouldn't say it. He wanted me to tell you he was dead. For your sake."

"Yes," she said slowly. "That would be like him. It is a long time now since they showed him to me. Is he . . . ?"

"He's all right," I said quickly. "Rotrox prisons aren't exactly pleasant places, but they leave him in peace now."

I wanted to ask her if Bec still called on her, but the words wouldn't come out. She rose and paced to the window, looking out blankly. Suddenly she turned, looking at me pleadingly.

"Couldn't you help him? Couldn't Becmath help him? He is

on good terms with the Rotrox. They might release him for him."

At that, I reflected, I could probably have tricked Imnitrin into sending Dalgo back to Rheatt with me. I could have told him I wanted him for myself. But I also knew that Bec would never stand for such a stunt.

"I'm sorry," I said. "Even if the Rotrox were willing — which they never will be — you'd never get Becmath to agree to it. You've tried, haven't you?"

She made a hopeless gesture. "Yes, I've tried, but not for a long time." She stood there, gazing at me sidelong, her eyes luminous. "How I hate that man! I don't understand you, Klein. You are a strong man. You are a born leader. Yet with Becmath you are weak. Why do you follow him like a pet animal? Why do you not defy him? I cannot believe that you fear him."

"There's no mystery," I said. "We both believe in the same things. That's why I follow him."

"He is evil, like the Rotrox."

I shook my head. "He's not evil," I said defensively. "He's a genius. Rheatt would be a lot worse off if it wasn't for him."

"Little he cares for Rheatt!"

There would be no point, I told myself, in trying to explain to her that Becmath worked not for himself, but for a higher ideal. Neither did I confess the doubts and anxieties that were beginning, despite myself, to eat into my guts.

Even before my trip to Merame we had begun setting up a baseline camp on the other side of the gateway. Most of our main equipment was already parked there: landsloops for street fighting inside Klittmann, big wagons for transporting food, fuel and ammunition, and a fleet of aircraft adapted for carrying heavy bombs so we could blast our way inside.

Bec planned a big role for aircraft in the new Killibol. He was quick to recognise that they could furnish the speedy communications the Dark World (to give it its ancient name) had so far lacked. City isolationism, as Bec called it, would shortly be at an end.

The two Rotrox legions were not long in coming. We pushed them through the gateway straight away to get them acclimatised. We didn't interfere with them in any way, but our own Rheattite forces were organised along different lines — in small units, Klittmann fashion, gangster fashion. We'd already taught them what to expect when they got inside the city.

I spent all my time on the other side getting things straightened out for the big drive. A few days later Bec and the others joined me. They were all eager for action.

The scene was vivid. Brilliant searchlight lit up everything. Neither the Rotrox nor the Rheattites could see too well in what was to them unrelieved gloom. During the time we spent at the base camp we were forced to wear our goggles just as if we had been on Earth.

The Rotrox, arrogant as usual, wished to be in the vanguard. I issued them with maps and they set off in their troop carriers with us following a few hours behind.

We crossed the river by the bridge we had built and set off across the dead landscape. The landsloops went first, in convoy, followed by the wagons and our own troop carriers. The command sloop, with me, Bec, Grale, Reeth and Hassmann in it, was the same one we had journeyed to Earth in; it was the only one that was atom-powered and it was larger than the others. During the rest period, when we camped, we slept in tents.

Usually we ate an evening meal with the top Rheattite officers headed by Heerlaw, our top man in the League of Rheatt. On our second day out a row blew up at one of these meals. The others had elected to eat on their own; neither Reeth, Grale nor Hassmann had ever become socially familiar with the Rheattites. Bec and myself sat with Heerlaw and half a dozen other officers comprising the effective leadership of their part of the campaign.

Earlier that day we had come across the remains of the handiwork of the Rotrox legions ahead of us. Evidently the Rotrox had stumbled on a band of nomads. The wagons and protein tanks were smashed open and strewn all over the place. Bodies were everywhere. It didn't look as if the Rotrox had left a single one of them alive.

"Is this the kind of civilisation we are bringing to Killibol?" one of the Rheattites denounced angrily. "Ever since I was a boy I have been hearing of the new vigour and freedom our work will bring to mankind. Is this what it means?"

This was strong stuff indeed. All the officers were young, belonging to the new generation we had raised. As he said, he'd been indoctrinated since he was a boy. To some extent they'd been quarantined from the real unpleasantness of Rheatt's position, or rather it had been played down to them. This was their testing time, their first exposure to nasty reality.

"From the Rotrox we must always expect brutality," Heerlaw answered, glancing at Bec. He was a man who wouldn't deviate no matter what he saw. He had been closest to us and he had the kind of toughness that's bred in Klittmann itself.

"We must co-operate with them for the sake of the task," he continued. "The end justifies the means."

Another officer broke in, slamming his knife on the table. "I say it was an atrocious act. It should be punished."

"Don't be a fool," Heerlaw told him. "How could the Rotrox have done otherwise? What if the people they found had sent word to the city we are about to attack?"

Throughout all this argument Bec sat silent. Suddenly I found myself speaking.

"You're right," I said. "It's sickening. If this is how we're going to behave it would be better if we had never set out. The Rotrox are monsters and it's not easy to imagine what will happen when they get inside Klittmann."

Bec glared at me fiercely. A brooding silence followed, in which the Rheattites continued to eat uneasily. Shortly afterwards we left for our respective tents.

Bec spoke to me warningly as we entered our own tent. "I don't want any disaffection in our ranks, Klein," he said, lowering himself into a comfortable chair and pouring us both goblets of *hwura*. "I think you spoke out of turn there."

"Maybe." I accepted the goblet. "But that guy had a point. Our Rheattites still aren't too hard-bitten. We've led them to believe they're going to build an empire worth building. Instead they see that mess we saw today. Frankly I'd be happier if the Rotrox were well out of this."

Bec snorted contemptuously. "I can remember when you wouldn't have turned a hair. Anyway, the Rotrox put us where we are. I'll handle them when the right time comes. Heerlaw has the right idea: the end justifies the means."

I knocked back the goblet and reached for the jug. "You haven't seen the things I saw on Merame."

We drank for a while. Bec was thoughtful. Finally he looked at me curiously and said: "I think you'd better make a trip back to Rheatt for a day or so, Klein."

The goblet stopped midway to my mouth. "Why?" I said in surprise.

"Those klugs were shooting their mouths off back there. I've had one or two indications back home — in Rheatt, that is — too. It could be there's an independence movement growing. Now would be the time for it to come into the open, when we're not around to stop it."

"But we'll soon be at Klittmann! I don't want to miss that."

"Oh, you won't, with any luck. Just nose around Parkland and see if everything's quiet. If there's nothing up you can fly out to Klittmann. Otherwise, you know what to do."

I was disappointed, but Bec was adamant. I had to go.

When I got to Parkland I soon got the feeling that Bec had given me a bum steer. Everything was as usual. The supply routes to the gateway were functioning perfectly. All the League of Rheatt organisations were waiting expectantly for news of the first victory.

Bec had told me to stay for at least two days, maybe three, I hung around, feeling moody and uncertain. There was no real need for me here. My mind was with those columns millions of light years away, pushing their way forward with headlights blazing.

Suddenly I thought of Harmen, the old alk. Bec and he had been close, in a way. Bec had got a lot of his ideas from him. Maybe it would be a good idea to talk to Harmen, I thought.

His laboratory was some distance from Parkland so I flew there in a small aircraft I piloted myself. I found Harmen sitting in a spacious study. In a small bookcase were the precious books he had managed to bring from Klittmann so many years ago.

On the way in I had noticed that the building was full of his assistants, or apprentices as he called them, wearing purple smocks. Harmen kept the house well lit for their benefit and wore dark goggles all the time. Otherwise he was the same crazy alk I had known before. His hair straggled down his shoulders and his big hooked nose poked out beneath the goggles, making him look like some weird animal.

I told him he'd soon be able to move back into Klittmann if he wanted to. He was non-committal. The move would be difficult, he said. Some of his equipment was heavy and conditions might not be stable in Klittmann for a while.

I got up and started pacing the room. Something was eating me but I couldn't put my finger on it.

"It's crazy!" I blurted suddenly. "When we got driven out of Klittmann you'd have sworn we didn't have a chance in hell. But Bec got us through the gateway and here to Earth — with your help, that is. Even then, you'd think we still didn't have a chance, except maybe just to stay alive. We were jumping into the dark. Yet here we are moving back to Klittmann with an army. In a few days we'll own the place. It just doesn't make sense."

Harmen nodded. He seemed to know what I was trying to say.

"Becmath is a man of destiny. That's why it happened. A lesser man taking such a chance would have landed in the middle of a desert. There would have been nothing for him. A man like Becmath lands in the middle of a whirlpool of events, of which he can take advantage. The universe denies him nothing."

I stared at him. "Why, you crazy loon. . . ." I shook my head. "All that philosophising is just junk. It doesn't mean anything."

The alk's mouth creased in a tolerant smile. "Indeed? And yet that is how the universe works. I know. I am close to the preparation of the Tincture."

I waved my hand. "Junk," I repeated.

"And the gateway — is that junk?"

He had me there. Then, too, I remembered the frightening little homunculus that had appeared in the retort under the garage in Klittmann. Harmen had proved he knew what he was talking about. If it was junk, then it was junk that worked.

"I can see that you are confused," Harmen said, his voice

becoming confidential. "Becmath's ambitions do not interest me except insofar as they help or hinder my work. But I can see what shape they take. Even when we were travelling over the barrenness of Killibol I knew that something was ahead that would enable Becmath to rise to power. I did not know what it would be, but I knew there would be something."

"But how could you know?" I said, fascinated now. "Did you have a premonition? A vision?"

He shook his head, smiling again. "I had merely studied the patterns events make. They are not what we take them to be: sometimes the effect draws on the cause."

He paused. "My life's work is the preparation of the Tincture. The Tincture, or the Primordial Hyle, is the basic material of existence of which all other elements and forms are corruptions or superficial appearances. Hence it is the goal of all alchemical work. It is indivisible, subtle and fugitive; it is not ruled by the laws of space and time. The ancient texts say that a man who possesses it can know all, can travel anywhere through space and time."

I remembered him making similar claims years before. Then, the meaning of what he said had been lost on me. Now I seemed to understand it better.

"You speak of visions," he continued. "I can give you visions. Come with me."

He rose and led me out of the study and into the laboratories beyond. Purple-smocked apprentices made way for us. We passed through one workshop filled with a confusion of electronic valves, retorts, and other stuff I couldn't begin to describe. Some of it was glowing and buzzing. Then, at the far end, big wooden doors swung open for us. We passed through and they closed again.

The chamber facing us was like a long hall, deathly quiet. It was empty except for electrode-like devices protruding from the walls, floors and ceiling at the far end.

"Preparation of the Tincture is the primary aim of alchemy," Harmen explained, "but there is another related, subsidiary aim: the creation of artificial beings. This apparatus goes a short way towards both."

He stepped to a control board and activated it with a loud

snap, then adjusted certain controls. The chamber began to hum.

"Do not be frightened by anything you see," he warned me. "Theoretically the Tincture is everywhere, at the basis of everything. All forms and creatures are derived from it — to obtain it, one merely has to make it manifest itself."

A sense of frightful tension between the electrodes began to make itself felt. My muscles began to tighten up. Instinctively I backed towards the door.

"Easy," Harmen murmured. "No harm will come to you."

Suddenly there was a sound like the clap of a giant electric spark. The space between the electrodes became a riot of colour. Then the spark coalesced into a tall figure — that of a man, dressed in bizarre, coloured clothes!

It was the figure in the retort all over again, but this time the creature was life-size — and undeniably real! His face was of a dark colour, almost black, which was offset dazzlingly by the crimson of his tunic and the whites of his eyes. His gaze lit on us and he began to walk towards us.

For a moment he seemed to rush towards me, growing bigger. Then he vanished, to be replaced by another figure between the electrodes, this time a woman dressed in simpler, green garments.

"Ignore them," Harmen murmured. "They are merely momentary creatures, produced spontaneously from the primitive Tincture by the field of stress."

The woman vanished and in her turn was replaced. The creatures began to stream off faster; then they came no more. The whine of power rose to a howl as Harmen poured in the energy from the control board. I felt myself sweating.

"We are approaching the threshold," Harmen said, his voice louder. "Now, Klein — behold!"

As he said that it was as if I had been sucked into some kind of vortex. I ceased to become aware of my surroundings. Momentarily I got a vivid sense of blackness, of being surrounded by stars and galaxies. I felt so stunned I could make no kind of reaction to it but merely let myself be carried along.

Then the impression of outer space vanished and I was looking down on the surface of Killibol. The advancing army was rumbling across the bare, level surface, sending a flood of light ahead of it.

All at once I seemed to see not just that one scene but the whole of Killibol together: the whole dead, slate-grey planet, with scores of cities like termite heaps none of which suspected what was to come upon them. At the same time images of Earth and Merame began to get jumbled up in it. And then my vision seemed to expand to include hosts of strange dramas on countless planets across the universe; Bec's saga was just one of them. I began to see what the alchemist had tried to tell me: that you can't always separate cause and effect. When the alchemists of ancient times had made that gateway between Earth and Killibol they had created more than a physical bridge; they had linked the two planets in other ways as well. Becmath, it seemed to me then, had been predestined to change the world he lived on since the moment he was born; he had been instinctively drawn towards the means of effecting that change as surely as, in some desert parts of Earth, certain animals are drawn to sources of water by some sense that cannot be explained.

There was a humming in my ears. The feverish visions passed. I was standing in Harmen's chamber amid the dying whine of power. Gasping, I wiped the film of sweat off my face.

"Is it real?" I breathed. "Or an hallucination?"

Harmen shrugged. "There may not be so much difference between the two. I prefer to say that it is real."

He opened the big wooden doors. Thankfully I staggered out. I didn't think I cared for the experience he had forced on me.

"And is that the Tincture you talk about?"

"No," he said, frowning. "It comes close to the reality of the Tincture — but in an extremely attenuated form that cannot be maintained. It is an ephemeral, partial manifestation of the Tincture brought about by extreme stress. Hence, like the corrupted Tincture of the gateway, it confers some of its properties — in this case visions of far-away events, and glimpses into the operations of matter in all its forms. To try to grasp it is like trying to grasp at air. Fully manifested Tincture is a palpable solid; it can be handled and made into an object."

Still breathing deeply, I glared around the bubbling laboratory. "That certainly must be something," I said. "You reckon you're going to make this stuff?"

"I believe I am close. The electric tension method I have just employed is not able to cross the final threshold . . . but we have other, more traditional processes under way." Harmen ran his fingers through his untidy hair with a hint of weariness. "To be frank, there is no reliable record that the final aim has been achieved by any man, except for the notable Hermes Trismegistus who became as a god. But no one doubts that the goal is attainable. And I am closer than anyone for many centuries."

He steered me between his watching apprentices and back towards his study. "There is something else of which I should in fairness warn you. You now possess a doppelganger."

"A what?"

"You remember the transient beings who came into existence as the field built up? You have been in contact, however remotely, with an attenuated Tincture field. I have found from experience that transient creatures fall away easily from such a field. There is now a phantasmal duplicate of yourself which will show itself in moments of extreme stress and for a short time after your death."

"I don't seem to remember asking for that!" I yelled angrily. All the bad stories I had heard about alks came flooding to my mind. I was ready to believe them, now.

But Harmen was unperturbed. "It will do you no harm. You won't even know about it, in all probability. I mention it only to forewarn you that Becmath also has a doppelganger."

"Bec?"

"Of course. He has always taken a close interest in my work. He also has gone through your recent experience. He drew great confidence from it."

In a strange way the visions I had been given, hallucinatory or not, had also given me confidence. Something had jelled in my mind. I felt more clear now about what was worth doing and what was not.

I flew back to Parkland and decided to rejoin Bec straight away. Ordering an aircraft to be readied to take me to the gateway, I went back to my private tower to clean up and get a change of clothes.

As soon as I stepped out of the elevator I stopped short. Grale was there. He was holding a handgun. Backing him up were two Rheattites of the League of Rheatt.

Grale grinned in his most unpleasant way.

"Hello, Klein. I've been waiting for you."

"What the hell are you doing here?" I demanded, going cold. "You're supposed to be on Killiboll."

"I'm pretty annoyed about that," he admitted, raising his eyebrows. "I wanted to be there when the fun started. But don't worry. There'll be plenty of laughs left when I finally walk in on dear old Klittmann."

"Does Bec know you're here?" I asked, measuring the distance between us.

Grale sniggered. His face looked even more greasy than I had ever seen it. "Bec sent me here, Klein. He figures you're getting soft. He wants you out of the way till the job's over."

So it was a bum steer after all. Bec had realised my indecision. Maybe he had thought I would foul things up for him.

"And you're the guy to do it, eh, Grale?" The old hatred between us flared in the air until it was almost red.

"Who else? I've waited twelve years for Bec finally to wise up to you. It's a real pleasure to see the roles reversed." Suddenly he snarled at the Rheattites: "O.K., you klugs, I'll handle it. Beat it." Then, remembering they didn't understand Klittmann, he repeated his instructions in faltering Rheattic.

As they left I edged along the wall. Grale was a pent-up spring, a frustrated killing machine. He was dangerous.

Alone with me, his grin became even wider. "You know something, Klein? Bec just wants me to keep you here cosy for a few days. So you can't go giving orders he doesn't like to those Rheattites you've nursed all these years. But why should I? Bec would understand if you raised objections. I might even have to kill you in self-defence. Then I could get back to the invasion."

I could hardly expect Grale to pass up this golden opportunity to get rid of me. He raised his handgun, his eyes shining and the lips drawn back from his white teeth. The knuckle of his index finger whitened.

Now I was opposite the blind covering the hole that, uniquely among the mobsters, I had included in the wall of my living quarters. I yanked back the blind, stepping aside.

Grale gave a yell as the sunlight flashed into his uncovered eyes. His bullet slammed into the wall beside me. He fired again, blindly. I was blind, too, but I wasn't dazzled. My eyes were closed. My gun was in my hand and I loosed off all fifteen shots in quick succession. Groping, I closed the blind.

Not all my shots had found their mark, but there were more than enough red stains on Grale's black jacket. He was as dead as he deserved to be.

I took a repeater from the arms cupboard, picking up a spare clip. The two Rheattites down below found the gun staring them in the midriff when I left the tower.

They backed away, consternation in their eyes. Very likely they had heard the gunfire and it unnerved them to see the white masters fighting among themselves.

"What were your orders?" I barked.

One shook his head. "We had no particular orders. We were to act as guards. The situation was not explained to us."

"Well, I'll explain it to you. The man upstairs is dead. He was trying to settle a private score, but I beat him to it. Does he mean anything to you?"

They shook their heads again. Grale was almost a stranger to them. I was the boss they were used to.

"All right," I said curtly. "Let's get back to Headquarters."

A few hours later I had flown to the gateway. The experience Harmen had given me was like a vivid dream overhanging everything, and I decided I was going to be near Bec for the next part of the proceedings, whether he wanted me there or not.

Fourteen

There were no aircraft at the base camp, and no pilots who knew the course. They were all outside Klittmann. The engineers had been putting down a landline so there would very shortly be television communication between Rheatt and Bec's army, but I didn't want to announce I was coming in case Bec got any more ideas about delaying me. So I hitched a ride on one of the supply wagons.

We took about eight days getting there. Already I was too late for the big fight.

The plain outside Klittmann was strewn with our wagons and a few parked aircraft, but evidently the sloops and the fighting men were already inside the city. The great grey pile of Klittmann was quite a sight: they'd bombed it heavily and one whole side of it was blasted open, masses of concrete having tumbled to the ground and the inside of the city being revealed in all its layer-upon-layer complexity.

I found my way inside the city, grabbed a Rheattite officer and went looking for Bec. The destruction inside Klittmann was unbelievable. Heavy explosives had been let off with criminal disregard for the buttresses that kept the whole place standing up. Prowling black sloops patrolled the dusty streets. The usual background noise of activity was absent, and in the silence I heard firing going on elsewhere in the city. It seemed that for the most part Klittmann was already in our hands. Many of the elevators had ceased working and we rumbled tortuously up ramps in one of the sloops, making for the upper levels where Bec had his headquarters.

Compared with the Basement where I had lived for so long before leaving Klittmann, the upper reaches we were now moving in were classy; but nearly ten years on Earth had dulled my appreciation of fine differences. Now it all looked sordid, montonous and claustrophic. Nothing but metal and concrete and stale, cold-smelling air.

There had been an awful lot of killing. At first I thought the Rotrox were the cause of that; but shortly before we reached Bec's hang-out we crossed a big plaza where I saw that Bec's revenge had been complete and vicious.

I made the driver stop the sloop and I got out to have a closer look. Piled in the plaza were bodies, their hands tied, riddled with bullet holes. Their fine dress told me they were high class: probably government members and tank owners.

More bodies hung by the neck from the overhead longerons. Dimly I realised that everybody whom Bec had looked on as an enemy in the past was here. I caught sight of Blind Bissey, the owner whose tank we had appropriated, swinging listlessly with eyes bulging, blind in death as they had been in life.

Bec had even killed Bissey's dog.

Wearily I climbed back in the sloop and signalled the driver to carry on.

When I walked in on Bec he was sitting in a fairly small, untidy office, a nearby table piled with papers. He was smoking a tube of weed meditatively. It was like old times.

If he was surprised to see me, he hid it. He scarcely moved.

"Hello, Klein. Didn't expect you so soon."

"So I believe," I said stonily.

I took a good look at him; as if seeing him for the first time: much smaller than me, a stocky, dapper body, the squared-off shoulders and dark, conservative Klittmann-style clothes; the square face and plastered-down black hair. The only big difference from ten years ago was that there was more jowl beneath the jaw.

He glanced up at me. "What happened to Grale?"

"He's dead. He tried to kill me, Bec. You should have sent another man to do the job. Or is that the way you wanted it?"

His gaze became speculative and distantly angry. "Whaddya mean he's dead? Who gives you the O.K. to go and wipe out Grale?"

"I've told you," I said evenly, "his idea was to wipe me out and tell you he was defending himself."

Bec listened while I told him the story of how I had tricked Grale with the blind. Finally he chuckled.

"Well, it looks like I had to lose one of you. Frankly, I'm glad it wasn't you. Care for a smoke?"

I took the tube he offered. It was the first in a long time.

"It looks like you have it all sewn up," I said, drawing the smoke into my lungs.

"That's right. It sure felt good to get even with some of the klugs running this place."

I wondered what had happened to all the philosophy Bec used to talk. Right now he seemed to be motivated by nothing but revenge. It gave me a bad feeling to see him gloat.

"Yes," I said, "I saw them on my way in. What happens next, Bec?"

"Things are going to move fast from now on. Very fast. I'll be needing your help, Klein. Right now we have Klittmann. We have very little time to knock it into shape. Because by the time a year is out we'll have damn near the whole of Killibol."

I held the smoke in my lungs for an astonished few seconds.

"But how?" It wasn't possible to conquer all the planet's cities, besieging them one by one, in anything like so short a time.

Bec's face became sardonic. "Technique, Klein, technique. It beats brute force every time."

"I don't see how any kind of technique is going to do what you're saying."

"Tank plague."

I couldn't have heard him right. I stared at him, puzzled and frightened. Ice began to congeal in my insides.

Tank and plague, when said together, are the two most terrible words on Killibol. More than one city had wasted away and died, destroyed by a famine nothing can relieve. Nobody ever visits the empty shell of such a city, not even centuries after.

But Bec was sitting here talking about it without batting an eyelid. "In Rheatt I had one or two projects going that I didn't tell you about," he said. "Maybe you heard about them indirectly. Anyway, while you were building up the League I got a few Rheattite scientists to work for me." He paused, lighting up another tube. "It's a funny thing. They're clever that way. But they never used any weapons like this against the

Rotrox. I guess they were scared it might get back to them. Anyway, they bred a special strain of tank plague, a disease that attacks the nutrient in the tanks but leaves protein and all animal life unharmed. I'm pretty sure there's no defence against it."

"So within a year there won't be a productive tank anywhere."

Bec nodded, giving me another glance with his glittering eyes. "It's beautiful. A virus. I've got agents flying out now to a dozen cities. They're wearing skin dyes so they won't look too strange. They've got orders to penetrate the cities — that's not too difficult for a man on his own — and release the virus. Once it gets into the air it has to get through to the tanks before long: there's no known filter that can keep it out. You realise what that means, Klein?"

"Sure." My throat was dry. "It means you're the master."

He was watching me carefully. "That's right. For some years I've been building up enormous stockpiles of food in Rheatt. The only food available on Killibol will have to come from Earth, through the gateway, which we control. Anybody who wants to eat will have to come to us. Things are going to have to be run as *we* say, and no other way."

But did Bec have enough food to feed *everybody*? I doubted it. Even granted that he couldn't get round to infecting every city in Killibol straight away, the population would still run into tens of millions, perhaps hundreds of millions. Perhaps he would set up tanks on Earth to produce protein faster than soil-grown food; but taking care of everybody he robbed of sustenance didn't seem to be uppermost in his mind right now.

"No," I said softly.

Something indefinable happened in his hard black eyes.

"What do you mean, Klein, no?"

I threw down the tube I was smoking. There was a feeling in my chest that seemed to be bursting. "That isn't the new state we talked of creating, Bec. You talked about freeing people from the slavery of the tanks. About breaking the stasis. Now you're putting a stranglehold on the cities that the tank owners could never even have dreamed of. How do you square that with everything you said, Bec?"

His right hand, resting on the table, shifted uneasily. "Don't be a klug. You have to be an iron man, a king, to achieve anything."

Bec was always a faster thinker than me. I could see I would have to get this over with quick. "I can't let you do it, Bec," I said. "I'm sorry. I didn't come so far with you for this."

He glared at me, his face raging.

"You punk! You trying to tell me how to run my own outfit?"

Keeping his glittering eyes on me, he got to his feet. Suddenly he lunged for his holster which was hanging on a hook on the wall. My gun was already in my hand. I fired once. The heavy slug caught him in the chest and knocked him sideways. He fell sprawling, face down, and didn't move.

I stood there, the gun still held stupidly in my hand, the blast still sounding in my ears. I felt lost, overpowered, like a son who has killed his father, or a dog that has killed its master. It was the first time I could remember that I had wanted to cry.

I believe I would never have seen it if it hadn't been for that mind-blowing experience in Harmen's laboratory. The visions I had seen there had expanded my mind and made me see things from a different angle. I saw clearly now that it wasn't any altruistic idea that had motivated Bec, but deeply selfish ambition. Valid though they were in themselves, the ideas he had taught me had been only means to establishing his own glory.

Perhaps he really had believed in them at one time; perhaps he had never ceased to imagine he still did believe in them. But towards the end he was too far gone for such claims to be credible. Had he lived, I could see nothing ahead for Killibol but an iron-jacketed tyranny.

"Hello, Klein."

The familiar flat baritone made my blood freeze. The side door was opening. Becmath stood there — *the same Becmath I had just shot and who was lying on the floor*!

Harmen's warning flashed into my mind.

Doppelganger!

Becmath moved into the room and turned over his own body with his foot, bringing the face into view. Then he looked up at me, wearing his usual sardonic smile.

"Looks like I underestimated you this once, Klein. Or maybe it was one of those subconscious mistakes Harmen talks about."

"Bec . . ." I tried to speak, but could only croak.

"Don't worry about it. I guess I did go slightly off the rails, didn't I? You can do it your way, now. Keep the boys in line, Klein. Don't let things get out of hand."

Suddenly he seemed to be advancing towards me, expanding to fill my vision, his smile growing more and more weird.

Then he was gone.

For what seemed like an age I did nothing but stand trembling. I became aware of the sound of running feet outside. Reeth burst into the room holding a repeater. He looked at me, then at Bec's corpse.

I stood him off with my handgun, trying to control myself. "I had to do it, Reeth. He was going too far."

"You mean the plague?"

I nodded. He stared in awe at the body, then slowly put up his gun.

"Yeah, it was pretty bad," he said with a sigh. "But the agents are already out. What are we going to do now?"

I let my own gun hand drop, the weapon hanging loosely in my fingers. Somehow I couldn't even find the strength to return it to my holster.

"We'll make out," I said. "We'll go along with Bec's original plan, the one he drew up years ago, and modify it according to circumstances. . . ."

Now that there was communication with Earth we could break the tyranny of the tanks once and for all, I thought. We could bring in any amount of fresh nutrient. We could import millions of tons of topsoil to grow natural food. At first some people might die due to Bec's meddling, but the situation would stabilise in time. There would be rapid air transit, between all cities. There would be commerce with Rheatt and the rest of Earth. It would be a two-planet empire where a man could act freely without fear of starving. As for the Rotrox, they would be dealt with.

Reeth shook his head regretfully. "And Bec promised me a dozen cities all of my own."

"You can have them," I told him. "There's going to be a

lot of organising to be done. But they won't be cities peopled
by slaves."

More footsteps sounded. Heerlaw came into the office,
backed by one of his countrymen. His eyes fell on Bec and the
thin ribbon of blood that was creeping across the floor; then at
the handgun that still hung limply in my fingers.

He stood stock-still before he spoke.

"You were right to kill him," he said at last. "For all his
genius, he was a man of blood and violence. But will you be
any better?"

"I hope so," I answered tiredly. "You'd better hope so, too,
because you can't do without me now."

That was true: Rheatt, the Rotrox, and now Klittmann,
were all joined in a contradictory web of hostility and mutual
support which would collapse into a gruesome bloodbath without someone to co-ordinate it. Bec had been that man, and I
was the only one who could step into his shoes. It was going
to take all my energy and skill to sort this mess out.

But then, I'd had the best of training.

There was one more thing.

The Klittmann tanks, naturally, had been the first to get hit
by the plague. As soon as the television landline was complete
I put through calls to Rheatt to locate the food stocks Bec had
mentioned. And after I had found them, I gave myself the
time to put through a call to Palramara.

Her face came up on the screen. The colours never seem to
come true on Earth television and her face had a pinkish,
rather than a green tinge. Briefly, if it's possible to put such
things briefly, I told her what had happened and that Becmath
was dead.

She received the news without any visible sign of emotion.
"And what now?" she asked.

Did she mean politics — or us?

Us. That was the problem I had been wrestling with since
I had killed Bec, when I hadn't been too occupied with more
important matters.

I knew I could have Palramara again if I wanted her. And
I did want her. With Bec out of the way we could come together again. The attraction was still there and it would still

work for us. But I also knew that I could get Dalgo off Merame if I tried hard enough. The choice was mine.

Her enlarged pupils stared at me distantly out of the screen. I swallowed.

"I'll do what I can to get your husband released," I said quickly. Her expression didn't change. I looked away.

"Goodbye, Palramara."

Abruptly I cut the connection.

I'd always been fairly lonely. I could be lonely again; it was no sweat.

For the thousandth time I wondered if Becmath's doppelganger had ceased to exist when it vanished, or if it had been drawn off into some other part of the universe. I hoped it had been annihilated, because I didn't like to think of him wandering around somewhere, lost and also alone.